A BLUEBIRD WILL DO

LOULA GRACE ERDMAN

Nancy Sullivan was only sixteen, but already she'd had adventures to last a lifetime. Her family had made the trip overland by wagon train from Illinois when everyone had "gold fever." Papa never made it to San Francisco, but Nancy and her mother buckled down and made a living there by serving meals.

And then her mother died, and Nancy was faced with a decision: to carry on alone, or try to hunt up Cousin Matilda in New Orleans. Veiled threats headed her back East, and this is the colorful story of her return trip across the Isthmus of Panama. It is filled with the people she encounters—Frank and Jim and mysterious Zeke, the menacing Courtneys, natives who mistake her for a witch doctor, and then of course, Rex Porter, someone Nancy found she could count on.

Aboard the *Mary Pearl* bound for Panama City, on muleback and then up-river in a *bungo,* it was just as the song said, "If you can't get a redbird, a bluebird will do." Likely it would turn out just as well—as it did for Nancy.

A Bluebird Will Do

Other books by Loula Grace Erdman

LOULA GRACE ERDMAN

A Bluebird
Will Do

DODD, MEAD & COMPANY · NEW YORK

ISBN: 0-396-06717-4
Library of Congress Catalog Card Number: 72-6881

Printed in the United States of America
by The Cornwall Press, Inc., Cornwall, N. Y.

For
Joe Ann Daly and Rosemary Casey
with appreciation

A Bluebird Will Do

Chapter 1

"... and you're all alone in the world," the woman said.

She twitters like a bird, Nancy thought. She even looks like one. A beak for a nose. Hair drawn up in wings on each side of her forehead. Talons for fingers. A vulture maybe, waiting to descend on me.

She had burst into the door, scarcely bothering to knock, calling, "Nancy! Nancy Sullivan. Here I am. I'm Mrs. Courtney. We live only a few doors down the street, and I just heard about your mother."

"Yes," Nancy said, looking out the window in the direction of the cemetery where Mama lay, flowers still fresh on the mound.

"Only sixteen years old," the woman, this Mrs. Courtney, said. "And all alone in the world." She shifted from one foot to another, showing no intention of leaving. "We moved in only a few days ago. The minute I heard about your mother, I knew I must come to you."

"That was kind of you," Nancy told her. "Won't you sit down?"

Mrs. Courtney took a chair, sitting on the edge of it. Nancy sat quietly in another chair, her hands folded in her lap. Tight, to keep them from trembling.

"So young, so pretty," Mrs. Courtney continued. "And rich, besides. You must not stay here alone."

"Not rich," Nancy corrected her quickly.

"Well, at least you have ample means." The woman spoke with the confidence of one who knows the facts.

Nancy let that pass without comment. Certainly she was no pauper. She did not need to ask anyone for help. Perhaps that was why she answered Mrs. Courtney so quickly and crisply.

"You must come home with me," the woman said. She got up from her chair quickly, and again Nancy was reminded of a bird ready to take flight. "Let's start packing your things. I'll help you."

"No!" Nancy's voice rose sharply. "No, I'm staying here."

"You mean in this house? Alone?"

"For the time being, yes."

"It isn't safe. All those rough miners hanging around town."

Rough miners, indeed. They were the ones who had made it possible for Mama and Nancy to stay here in San Francisco. They were the ones who had stood by at the last, and made the coffin and dug the grave. Yes, and even brought wild flowers to place on it. They had found a minister who said the words for the final service. They had been here this morning, when Nancy needed them. Why hadn't Mrs. Courtney been with them, if she was all that anxious to help?

Naturally Nancy couldn't tell her this. Instead, she said, "I know there are rough ones, but there are also some good ones. They were our friends. They helped us. They helped me." Her voice broke slightly, remembering.

"Even so, you can't stay here by yourself," Mrs. Courtney said. "You must come home with me. We'll put a cot in the front room for you. Mr. Courtney told me I was to bring you." She spoke as if that made the whole thing final and sure.

Again Nancy looked in the direction of Mama's grave. Only this morning they had put her there. Then Nancy had come home, back to the house so empty and strange without Mama. She had given no thought as to what she was going to do next. Except she was very sure she wouldn't go with Mrs. Courtney.

"I'm staying here," she said flatly. "At least, for the present."

"But how?"

Nancy stood up, indicating that as far as she was concerned the call was over. She knew Mama would have thought this most impolite of her, but how else was she to convince Mrs. Courtney there was no use talking any more about the matter?

"I'll manage," Nancy told her. "And now, if you'll excuse me, I have a great many things to do."

Mrs. Courtney stood too, and then moved toward the door. Once there, she stopped, evidently planning to continue her argument.

"Good-by," Nancy said. She didn't add, "Thank you for coming," because she really wasn't grateful, even for the offer of a place to stay. Then feeling guilty and knowing she had been rude, she added, "It was thoughtful of you to ask me to stay with you."

Mrs. Courtney, at the door now, turned to face Nancy. "I still don't see how . . ." she began.

"I'll work things out," Nancy told her.

The visitor walked out of the door, closing it behind her.

"I'll manage," Nancy told herself, saying the words aloud as if that made them more emphatic. "I'll manage."

And she would. For the last few months her life had been made up of learning to manage.

Back in Illinois, where they had lived before coming to California, things were different. There it was Papa who took over, always laughing and happy and full of jokes. He would make some outrageous, impractical plan, and then break into a song or an Irish jig. "It's straight from County Clare I am," he would say. "It's from me Nancy gets her black hair and blue eyes." And Mama would say,

"Oh, Clarence," and laugh with him. Anything Papa did was fine with her.

Sometimes Papa would lapse into Spanish. *"Buenos días,"* meaning "good day"; or *"amigo,"* which was "friend"; or *"sí,"* which was "yes."

He spoke Spanish—not much, but a little—because the freighter on which he left Ireland docked in Mexico. That was all right with Papa. He wanted to see the world. He stayed long enough to learn a bit of Spanish and then went on to New Orleans where he had a cousin, Matilda Hogan.

"And a wonderful woman she is," he often said. "If ever you need help, she'd be the one who would give it to you, and gladly."

He didn't stay very long in New Orleans. A boat was going up the Mississippi River, and he decided he'd go too, and see more of this new world. At St. Louis he got off and started east, into Illinois. It wasn't long before he came to Welton, the little hamlet where Mama lived. She was an orphan, with no close relatives, at least none that she knew about. She had been brought up by some kind people who took good enough care of her, and when they died, only a short time before Papa came along, they left her the store which they had run.

Mama knew almost nothing about the business; her foster parents had never given her any responsibility. They didn't take the store too seriously themselves, evidently, for they rented the building which housed it, having their living quarters upstairs.

She was thinking about going somewhere else—maybe away to school—when along came Papa. Only, of course, he wasn't anybody's papa then, just as Mama wasn't anyone's mama.

"The minute I saw Anna I knew straightaway that I wanted no more of the wandering life," Papa would often say, looking fondly at Mama. "So I set about trying to persuade her to marry me."

He was so successful in this that they were married, and together ran the store. Immediately business began to thrive. People came to buy, but did not leave once their purchases were completed, because they were enchanted with Papa's stories and his gay good humor. Since they stayed longer, they bought more. Sometimes it was mealtime before they thought of leaving. Then Papa would say, "Why don't you have a bite with us?"

Mama never minded. She was an excellent cook and always had more than enough food. She enjoyed seeing the people who came in.

By and by Nancy was born.

"Never was there a more beautiful baby," Papa often said.

When she was small, Nancy took the statement for granted, not thinking much about it one way or the other. Since there were no children in the few families living in Melton, she had no way of comparing herself with others her own age. Then, almost overnight as it were, she was sixteen and nearly as tall as Mama.

"Gets more beautiful every day," Papa would declare proudly.

His words sent Nancy to the mirror to check what she saw there. Yes, her hair was black and slightly curly, like Papa's. She brushed it carefully, parted it in the middle, and smoothed it down, letting ringlets hang softly against her cheeks. Her eyes were like Papa's too. Blue, with thick black lashes. Her skin was fair, her cheeks faintly pink. She reached up to touch her face gently with her long-fingered, slender hands. She knew Papa would love her, no matter what she looked like. Even so, she was glad the image she saw reflected in the mirror reassured her that he was not entirely wrong when he talked about the way she looked.

Immediately after Nancy's birth, Papa wrote Cousin Matilda Hogan, back in New Orleans, to tell her about the new baby, just as he had written when he married Mama.

"We've named her Nancy Matilda," Papa told her.

Cousin Matilda wrote back that she was delighted. Down the years she and Papa continued their correspondence. Her letters were always kind and cordial. You could tell she truly loved Papa and was prepared, because of that, to love Mama and Nancy too.

Nancy practically grew up in the store. Her earliest memories were of playing there while Mama and Papa waited on customers, measuring out lengths of cloth, weighing coffee or sugar or flour. She could remember sitting on a cushion back of the counter, poring over the books Papa found for her.

"Must feed the mind as well as the body," he would say.

There was no school in the tiny hamlet where they lived, the nearest one being some five miles away. Papa said he'd teach her himself, which he did, taking her through nursery rhymes and fairy stories, going on to whatever books happened to be around the house. For the most part, these were the ones Mama had used when she herself was in school. Papa especially enjoyed geography, always acting pleased when he could say of some place they were discussing, "I've been there. 'Tis very much as the book says."

He spent less time on arithmetic.

"Your sums you can learn helping in the store," he said, "adding up grocery bills."

Occasionally people didn't want groceries. Instead, they would say to Mama, "I'm not feeling so good, Mrs. Sullivan. How about a dose of your medicine. Will you sell me a bottle?"

"Oh, my goodness, no," Mama would tell them. "Here . . . take this with you."

She would fill a small bottle with dark liquid, a concoction she brewed from juices of herbs, boiling it on the kitchen stove, watching it carefully, a look of deep concentration on her face as she did so. The recipe, which she said had come down from her foster mother, was "in her head," and she never wrote it out either for herself or anyone else. The people who took the medicine seemed to feel better, and said so.

"We don't need a doctor in town, with you here," they told Mama.

They didn't need a newspaper either, with the store. Someone was always coming in to tell about the latest happenings in the community, in the state, or even in the nation. That's how the Sullivans found out about the event that was to change the pattern of their lives.

A man who was passing through stopped to buy groceries. "Have you heard?" he asked. "Gold! They've discovered gold. A place called Sutter's Mill. In California."

"Gold!" people echoed. "Just to think of it! Gold. . . ."

They talked as if it might be over the hill, maybe in the next township.

Before long, wagons full of people began to come through the town. Single ones. Groups of them. Men riding horseback, even a few walking. They all said they were going to California, where gold nuggets were lying on the grass, thick as dandelions in a field. Streams were yellow with pure gold. All a body needed to do was hurry out and get his share. Gold belonged to the person who found it. There was no law to stop you from scooping it up.

"Wagon trains leave regularly from Independence, Missouri," they said. "It's better to be with a group. Safer."

They bought provisions and pushed on.

"Gold fever," Mama sniffed, watching them leave. "Wonder if there's any cure for it."

Finally, Papa said what Mama must have known he would.

"Anna, I'm going to California," he told her.

"And leave us?"

"Of course not. You'll go too. It will be a great adventure. The trip will be good for Nancy. Give her a chance to see a different world. After all, she's sixteen, and has scarcely been out of this town. Now when I was her age . . ." He waved his hands toward the horizon, indicating the wide range of his travels.

"It's different for girls," Mama told him.

"Travel is good for anyone," Papa declared. "Makes them grow."

Mama didn't really try to talk him out of going. Perhaps she knew it was no use. Anyway, whatever Papa wanted to do was all right with her. And Nancy was delighted with the idea. California. Gold! It sounded magic and wonderful beyond all telling.

"All right," Mama said. "We'll go with you."

"Oh, Mama!" Nancy brought the words out, breathless with delight.

They began preparing for their journey. Papa had Jake Collins, the blacksmith, attach bows to a wagon. Together, they stretched canvas across them. He bought a team of mules from a farmer.

"Tougher than horses," Papa said.

One day Papa came home with some news. "Collins wants to buy the store," he said.

"We don't own the building," Mama reminded him. "We rent."

"Oh, he knows that," Papa told her. Which, of course, he did. Everybody here knew everything about his neighbors. "He wants to buy the groceries and other supplies in it. Thinks he'd like to run a store himself. Rather, have his wife keep it while he stays in the shop."

"Well," Mama said, going along with Papa's idea the way she always did, "it suits me all right. I'll pack the wagon with the things we'll need on the trip. He can have what's left."

"I'll tell him," Papa said. "Matter of fact, I have already halfway promised him that we'd trade him what we leave in the store for the canvas and the work he did on the wagon."

So Mama, with Nancy to help her, began packing food and other supplies into the wagon bed. Dried fruits. Beans. Coffee, tea, and sugar. Salt and pepper. Molasses. Salt pork and hams. Lard. Potatoes, both Irish and sweet. Flour and corn meal.

"All this food," Papa marveled. "What are you going to do with it?"

"We can't eat gold," Mama told him calmly.

She put in her sewing kit, with its spools of thread and

needles and scissors and such. She also packed a box of matches. Magic things, these, and not easy to come by. You struck the head of one across a rough surface, and then there was a small flame, ready to light a fire.

She washed bedding and their clothes.

"You and I will each have a trunk," Mama told Nancy. "Papa is putting his things in a box. Pack your good dresses in the bottom. We won't need them going overland."

Nancy folded her favorite dress, the flowered challis with its flat lace collar and fitted bodice. She placed it in the trunk. With it she put her lace mitts and a soft shawl. The dresses to be worn on the trip, together with sturdy knitted shawls, were laid on top of the pile. Nancy even found room for a few of her books.

Mama packed her own trunk quickly, not seeming to give much thought to what she took. She was more concerned about finding room to tuck in bottles of her medicine among the other cargo the wagon held.

"Just in case," she said.

They started off early one morning in April. Spring was a good time to begin the overland trip, people said. The mules could feed on roadside grass.

Mama and Papa sat on the wagon seat and Nancy on a pallet just behind it. At night, that was to be Nancy's bed while Papa and Mama's would be at the back of the wagon.

Friends stood in doorways, waving good-by to them. Nancy, from her place in the wagon, watched them until the road turned and she could see them no longer.

In due time they came to Independence. It was as Papa had said. Wagons were lined up at the river, waiting to cross, ready for the first stage of the journey across the plains, over the mountains, until at last they would come to California.

It didn't take Papa long to start talking with the people in those waiting wagons. He came back to report to Mama.

"A big party left yesterday," he said. "Another one is going as soon as they can be ferried across the river. I was talking to some people and they said we could join them. Let's go over and meet them."

He led the way, Mama and Nancy following him. Papa made the introductions. First, they met the Morgans. "My wife," Papa said, "and my daughter, Nancy. Meet Mr. and Mrs. Morgan and . . . and . . ." He hesitated, seeing a little boy standing beside Mrs. Morgan.

"Our son, Don," Mrs. Morgan told them.

"I'm six," the boy said.

Mama said, "How do you do," very proper and right. Nancy could tell she liked Mrs. Morgan and would have enjoyed staying there to talk with her. But Papa was already on his way to the next wagon, Mama and Nancy accompanying him.

"Mr. and Mrs. Coates," Papa told Mama.

Mrs. Coates said, "Howdy," and Mr. Coates, sitting on the ground near the wagon nodded, not bothering to get up, spoke too.

"He don't feel so good," Mrs. Coates explained. "He got sick after we left home, back in Indiana." She was a huge, gaunt woman, looking much larger, older, and certainly stronger than her husband. "We're hoping the climate in California will help him."

A man walked over to them. He was grizzled, a little shabby, but had a kind and gentle smile. "Name's Baker," he said. "Bill Baker. I'm traveling alone."

Mama spoke to him politely, and he said, "Howdy, Ma'am," and then turned to Papa. "I've worked with a bunch of freighters and I been over part of this trail before. You ought to trade off them mules for a couple of yokes of oxen. They stand the trip better."

"But I thought . . ." Papa began.

"You can trade here," Bill Baker said. "A man over there sells them."

Papa looked around at the waiting wagons. Sure enough, most of them did have oxen standing patiently, waiting to leave.

"All right," Papa agreed. Together, he and Bill Baker went over to make the trade.

And the next morning, a yoke of oxen drew the wagon and another pair trailed along behind. "They take turns pulling the wagon," Bill explained, "so as not to wear them out." They were ferried across the river and were on their way.

There were twenty or more wagons in the party, but Mama, Mrs. Morgan, and Mrs. Coates were the only women. Perhaps that was why their wagons formed a sort of unit of their own. Bill Baker chose to throw in with them, giving advice now and then about how things should be done.

From the very first, Mama and Mrs. Morgan got along, talking with each other freely and easily.

"I didn't want to come," Mrs. Morgan confided. "It's not easy, going across overland, I hear. There'll be rivers to cross, and mountains, and the desert. And," she lowered her voice, apparently not wanting Don to hear, "Indians. Although, I understand they are friendly for the most part."

"Yes," Mama said, not so much agreeing with her as encouraging her to continue.

"It could take us five months, maybe, although Mr. Morgan insists we'll make it in three." She paused, obviously thinking what could happen to them during those months, and then she went on. "But Tom insisted, and I finally gave in."

"Well, it wasn't my idea, either," Mama admitted. "You know how men are."

They nodded their heads in sympathetic agreement, but Nancy felt sure neither of them would have changed things. Mrs. Morgan evidently went along with everything Mr. Morgan wanted, just the way Mama did with Papa.

Mrs. Coates was different. She took charge herself, driving the team of oxen, looking after them when it was time to make camp at night, yoking them the next morning. For the most part, Mr. Coates lay on a pallet in the wagon. Some of the men offered to help Mrs. Coates, but before long they quit doing this, perhaps realizing she was a little embarrassed to have them offer.

It was young Don who became Nancy's good friend.

"I like you," he said at the end of the first day when they were camped by a small stream for the night. "You're pretty."

"Oh, thank you," Nancy told him.

"Let's go down to the water," he said. "Maybe we can find some birds' nests or something."

"Sure," she agreed. And together they started down the path.

It came to her that she really knew little about children. As far as that went, she didn't know young people her own age. Most of her life had been spent with Papa and Mama and their friends.

"Watch out for snakes," Bill Baker called after them.

"Yes," Nancy said, wishing he hadn't warned them. It almost spoiled the walk. But she realized he was right, and so kept to the open path, watching carefully. They didn't see any birds' nests, but they did come back with some flowers.

The women were cooking over a joint campfire. Mama had gone into her stores in the wagon, bringing out choice bits of ham and dried fruit and other good things. These she offered to share.

"Now listen," Bill told her, "you keep that stuff stored away. We have to live off the country as much as possible on the way out. Got a long trip ahead. Don't use your own stuff until you have to."

Mama seemed to realize he was right. After that, she hoarded her supplies. They cooked game the men shot, or fish brought from the streams near which they camped. They picked berries from wayside bushes, always taking the advice of Bill as to whether these foods were safe. He was a great help to them, as Papa and Mr. Morgan agreed.

"It's better than I thought it would be," Mrs. Morgan acknowledged. "Only thing, I hate for Don not to be in school. He would have started this year."

Suddenly Nancy remembered the books packed in the wagon. "Would you . . . I mean, Don and I could have lessons together . . . if you like," she added hastily.

"Oh, thank you, thank you," Mrs. Morgan said. "If you only would."

So Nancy started Don on lessons. At first, she did little but tell him stories, or read aloud to him. He would crawl into the Sullivan wagon and sit beside her while the oxen plodded along. Having him there helped to break the monotony.

One day he looked at the book she was reading. "I know that word," he told her. "I've seen it lots of times when you read to me. It's *the*." He put his finger on the word.

"Why of course it is," Nancy told him. "Now let's see how many others you know."

Before long Don was reading. First single words, and then sentences. Slowly, and not always correctly, but at least making progress. Mrs. Morgan was delighted.

"I can't thank you enough," she said.

Nancy, too, was pleased. Who knows, she thought, maybe some day I'll be a teacher.

The wagons pushed on, the oxen plodding along, never varying their pace, rarely seeming tired. Bill had been right in urging Papa to trade for them. They gave no trouble. There were other things, however, Nancy found not so pleasant about the trip. For instance, the howling of the wolves and coyotes at night, often at the very edge of their camp. A truly chilling sound it was, and Nancy found herself drawing back instinctively from the wild chorus.

"They won't hurt you," Bill consoled her. "They are more afraid of you than you are of them." Even so, she never quite became accustomed to the sounds.

There were other necessary parts of the journey which she always dreaded. One was getting across the streams and rivers on the road they must follow. At times the water was shallow enough so that the team could be driven through it. Often they had to pay a ferryman to take them across. Occasionally the oxen were unyoked and made to swim across while the wagons were ferried. Nancy never quite let herself breathe until everyone was safely on the other side.

They snaked their way over mountain passes. Here Bill was a great help, having traveled the road before and knowing the best paths to take. Even so, managing the rocky, rugged route was not easy. Sometimes fallen rocks blocked their path. At such times the men had to get out and help clear the way before they could go on. It was easy to understand why people said going with a party was the best way to travel.

There were other experiences, even more grim. One day they passed a freshly-made grave by the side of the road. On a crude wooden slab were carved the words, "Sam Gilmore. Aged 22. Rest in peace."

"Poor boy," Mrs. Morgan said softly. "I wonder . . ." She did not finish, but Nancy knew what she meant. She herself was wondering what had happened. Perhaps the same thing lay in wait for them, somewhere down the road they were traveling.

As they went on, they began to see all sorts of articles lying beside the road. Pieces of furniture first. "Should have known better than to start out with them. Have to travel light, going west," Bill said.

Farther along there were other grimmer testimonies to the hardships of the road. Carcasses of dead animals, either skeletons or decomposing bodies lying in grotesque positions. Oxen. Mules. Even a milk cow now and then. Seeing them, Bill said thoughtfully, "I think we better walk when we can. Save that much strain on the teams."

So Nancy and Mama, Mrs. Morgan and Don got out and walked beside the wagons. Occasionally Mr. Morgan and Papa and Bill joined them, driving the teams ahead of them. Mr. Coates stayed in the wagon, with Mrs. Coates driving and making no explanation for his failure to walk with the others. Nancy, her own feet sinking into the roadside dust, wondered briefly if Mr. Coates wasn't about the smartest one of them all.

They were getting into dust now. It was everywhere. In their shoes, in their clothes, in their bedding. Particles of it in the food they cooked over campfires. It covered a pile of discarded articles lying at one side of the road.

"Aren't they . . . ?" Don asked curiously.

"Leave them alone," Mrs. Morgan cried nervously. "They are guns!"

And they were. But they were so broken apart, so battered up, that even Nancy could see they would harm no one. Perhaps would never be of any use again.

"They won't hurt him," Bill reassured Mrs. Morgan. Then in an aside meant only for the men, he explained, "That's to keep the Indians from using them."

But Nancy heard him and felt a chill of fear. Mrs. Morgan had been right in fearing the possibility of encounters with Indians as one of the dangers of the road.

Occasionally they did see Indians, sometimes a group of them watching silently from a spot at some distance from the train. Now and then a few of them drifted into the camp. But they seemed to mean no harm. Still, Nancy could not get all those stories out of her mind, the ones about the killing, the scalping, the robberies, and worse. She remembered the useless guns back at the roadside. Bill was not discounting the dangers of Indian attack either.

Now and then they met a wagon headed east.

"Decided she couldn't take it," the man would say, pointing to his wife. The woman rarely answered, probably not caring so long as she was getting her way and going back home.

If Mama or Mrs. Coates or Mrs. Morgan wanted to join those eastbound wagons, they never said so.

"See any Indians?" Bill asked the man in the first wagon they met.

"Well, not really. Just results. They had pretty well wiped out a wagon train not too far ahead of us. Then a bunch of men got together and gave them a real hard time. Killed most of them, I heard. Seems that taught them a lesson. Understand they've quieted down and aren't giving any trouble now. Of course, nobody knows when they'll break out again. . . ."

"Can't say I blame them," Bill said. "White men coming out and killing off the buffalo. There's where Indians get their food, to say nothing of hides for tents and clothing."

When a few days later, the wagons came to the grazing herds of buffalo, Nancy wondered why the Indians thought anyone could ever make a dent in the seemingly unending numbers of the great shaggy beasts. They grazed for miles on both sides of the trail, standing so close together they seemed to be a part of the landscape itself.

Some of the men in the party shot one. Choice portions, roasted over the campfire, tasted so delicious that Nancy could understand why the Indians did not wish the supply to be endangered.

The wagons went on. They stopped briefly at Fort Bridger, resting for the next stage of the journey. They went on to Salt Lake, where the Mormons had gone before them. They crossed the desert, an experience Nancy tried to block from her memory. Heat, and the sun blazing down on them as they walked along, and always the lack of water and the great fear that maybe there would be none at all farther along the road. But they came through that too.

"Know what," Bill Baker said one evening. "Near as I can make out, everyone in this train is going to Sutter's Fort. That's where they first found the gold. Bet that place is so thick with gold hunters you can't put down a shovel. I got another idea."

"What is it?" Papa and Mr. Morgan asked. During the trip they had grown to respect Bill's judgment.

"I say it would be better to go to San Francisco and fan out from there. Wouldn't have so much competition."

And that is what they did. Their four wagons left the main party, probably scarcely being missed.

"Way I figure it," Bill said, "three, four weeks we'll be there." He made it sound as if it was no time at all.

One day they came to a spot they all found enchanting. A ravine, with trees at the bottom and a small stream flowing bright and clear. Paths led to it, well worn by the feet of the animals that had been taken down to drink. Grass, green and lush, grew on the banks.

"How about stopping here," Papa suggested.

Bill and Mr. Morgan said it was a fine idea, even if it was only noon. A rest would be good for all of them.

"The oxen can stay down there until morning," Bill said, "filling up on that good grass."

They unhooked their teams, and, without any objection from Mrs. Coates, took hers with them as they started toward the edge of the ravine. Nancy and Don tagged along, just to have a closer look at the lovely spot. After the desert, water was a wonderful thing to see.

Papa went first, leading the Sullivan oxen. He came to the edge of the ravine where the path to the water started. At its edge was a small projection covered with dense underbrush, and overhanging the ravine itself. It all happened so fast that afterwards nobody could give a really accurate account. Just as Papa was directly in front of the underbrush, a furry mass fairly exploded from its depths. It was a coyote, evidently terrorized because it thought Papa was blocking its escape. Through Nancy's dazed mind Bill's words came back. "Lot more afraid of you . . ."

In its wild dash to escape, the animal collided with Papa, hitting him squarely on the shoulder. Papa, caught completely off guard, grabbed at the oxen bridle, trying to maintain his balance. He missed and reached again, but could not grasp the bridle. Instead, he toppled over the edge of the ravine.

There was the sound of his body falling, of rocks dislodged as he went down, of the horrified gasp of the other men, and Mama's screams. Then, finally, there was Papa, lying at the foot of the ravine.

The men made a packsaddle with their hands to bring him back to the top. Blood poured from an ugly cut in his scalp. Mama rushed toward him, and he tried to speak to her, only it was difficult because there was blood coming from his mouth as well.

"Put him here," Bill said, stopping beside the wagon.

"Not on the ground!" Mrs. Morgan cried. She ran to her own wagon and brought back a sheet which she spread on the ground. The men placed Papa on it, gently, and then stepped back to make way for Mama who came to where he lay, dropping on her knees beside him. Nancy knelt with her, wanting to help, too stunned even to cry.

"It's the end for me, Anna darling," Papa whispered, speaking with great difficulty.

"Let's not even talk like that . . ." Mama said, her voice breaking.

"I know . . ."

She reached out and took his hand. He didn't speak again. Finally Mr. Morgan and Bill came over, touched her on the shoulder, and told her what she must have already guessed. Papa was dead.

"Oh, darling, darling . . ." Mrs. Morgan sobbed, coming over to take Mama in her arms.

Mama acted as if she didn't even hear her. As, perhaps, she didn't.

They buried Papa there by the side of the road, not far from the ravine which had been responsible for his death. Mrs. Morgan found some roadside flowers to put on the grave. Mr. Morgan read from his Bible and said a prayer. Afterwards, he and Bill erected a small wooden slab with Papa's name and age carved on it.

By the time they were finished, it was dark and they all looked around hesitantly, knowing it was time to turn in, but not quite sure what to do about it. Finally Mr. Morgan said to Mama, "Best we go to bed. We should leave in the morning. You know that, don't you?"

Mama nodded, although Nancy doubted if she really heard him or, hearing, realized what he was saying. But she did go to the wagon, Nancy following her.

Mama made no move to take out the bedding that had been hers and Papa's all the way. Instead, she went over and, without even undressing, lay down on Nancy's pallet.

Nancy looked at her uncertainly. "Mama," she said, "it's time to go to bed."

Mama did not answer.

Nancy considered the situation for a moment and then went to Mama's trunk and found her nightgown. "Here," Nancy said, handing it to her.

Mama, still acting as if she didn't know what she was doing, put on the nightgown. Then she stretched out on the pallet once more.

After a moment's hesitation, Nancy undressed, got into her own nightgown, and lay down beside Mama. She couldn't go to sleep, though. It didn't seem real that Papa wasn't with them. The events of the day began to rush past her, like leaves dancing in the wind. Beside her, Mama seemed to have dropped off into a troubled sleep. Then, quickly, she called out. "Clarence—"

The sound of her voice frightened Nancy for a moment, and then she realized Mama was talking in her sleep.

Mama reached out and touched Nancy's hand lightly, as if to reassure herself.

"Nancy . . ." Mama said. The girl could tell by the way she spoke that she was still not awake.

But *I* am awake, Nancy thought. And suddenly things came clear to her. Mama had always depended on Papa for everything. Now Papa was gone. But she, Nancy, was left. She reached over and patted Mama's hand.

"Yes, Mama," she said. "I'm here."

It didn't matter that Mama was asleep. Nancy was really talking to herself, anyway.

The next morning when the party started off, it was Nancy who sat on the side Papa had occupied. It was she who held the lines, guiding the oxen and heading them west toward San Francisco.

Chapter 2

THEY CAME to San Francisco late one afternoon, the wagons in the same formation they had used since Papa's death. Bill first, with Mr. and Mrs. Coates next. Behind them Mama and Nancy, with the Morgans bringing up the rear.

Bill halted at the edge of what appeared to be a camp. Tents were pitched on the sandy ground; wagons stood around in no set pattern. People milled about restlessly, like birds halted briefly in flight before taking off to some other destination. A man was cooking over a small campfire, close to where Bill's wagon had stopped. He looked up and said, "Howdy," sounding as if, even with all these people around, he was lonesome.

"Do we need to get permission to camp here?" Bill asked the man.

"No, you don't have to ask. Just pitch camp. Unless you have some place else to go, which I doubt. Town's jumping with people. No hotel room, even if you had the money to pay for it. I reckon you're on your way to the Diggings."

"The Diggings?" Mr. Morgan asked.

"Yep. Out where they dig for the yellow stuff. Won't find any here. Leastways, not much. That's not to say people aren't getting rich in this town, charging seven prices for everything they sell."

"Think we might as well make camp here?" Bill asked Mr. Morgan.

And Mr. Morgan said yes, it seemed all right.

"We'll look after the teams," Bill said to Mama and Mrs. Coates.

Nancy could understand the reason for the offer. Among all the people camped here, scarcely a woman was in sight.

They unyoked the oxen and started off to the stream to water them. Nancy looked about her, beyond the place they were camped, toward the town of San Francisco itself. In the distance, mountains rose blue against the sky. Buildings, some adobe, some wooden, hugged the water. Some of these were substantial looking, but others apparently had been thrown together in a great hurry.

This is the end of the journey, she thought, the place we have been pushing toward ever since we left home. It doesn't seem real that we are here. But after Papa's death, nothing had seemed real. Not to Nancy and certainly not to Mama, who had walked about like someone in a daze, neither believing nor accepting what had happened. The only time she was anything like her old self was when the group made camp and she and Mrs. Morgan and Mrs. Coates began preparing the evening meal. Perhaps, Nancy thought, this was because then she was on familiar ground. Cooking was Mama's link with the life she had once known.

Now they were in San Francisco, or at least, at the edge of it. California had been Papa's dream, but he was not here to share it. Mama must have been thinking of this, as Nancy was. Mrs. Morgan and Mrs. Coates were both taking out cooking utensils, making ready to prepare a meal. Mama stood, looking vaguely off toward the blue waters of the Bay. I have to get her out of this some way, Nancy thought. And then an idea came to her.

"Mama," she said, "I'm hungry."

Mama came to life at the words. "Yes. I know. What would you like to have?" she asked.

"Ham," Nancy told her. It would be a touch of home, something they had brought with them.

"That sounds good," Mama agreed, seeming to be grateful for the suggestion. "And potatoes with it?"

"Yes," Nancy said. "Mrs. Morgan and Mrs. Coates brought their wood from that pile over there. I'll get some for us, so we can build a fire."

There were, indeed, scraps of wood lying on the ground, perhaps left by campers who had taken off before they had time to use it. Nancy walked over to collect some of it and when she came back, Mama was bringing out the little iron grate, the one they had used during their trip. She put it on the ground, and struck one of the precious matches to light a fire with the wood Nancy had brought. When it was burning to suit her, she brought supplies from the wagon. Slices of ham, potatoes, coffee, and cooking utensils. Without question, Nancy picked up a bucket and started toward the stream.

"I'm going with you," Don announced.

Nancy said, of course, she'd love to have him. They walked off together, the boy keeping up a constant stream of comments. When they came back, he went to his own wagon and Nancy to hers. Mama was putting some slices of ham into the skillet.

Bill and Mr. Morgan brought the oxen back, and tied them securely with their own teams. "We'll keep looking after them," Bill promised, and Mama said she was very grateful to them.

"You can peel the potatoes," Mama told Nancy. "Here's a pan to put them in. I'll make coffee."

Nancy began peeling the potatoes, thinking how good it was to have Mama acting more like herself again.

Presently two men, young, lean, bearded came by. They stopped close to the wagon, hesitated, and finally walked over to Mama.

"Howdy-do, Ma'am," they said.

"Good evening," Mama said. She went on with the business of cooking, turning slices of ham carefully, lifting the lid of the potato kettle and using a fork to test their doneness. The young men still stood there, watching her as she worked. By now the smell of coffee was beginning to mingle with the other cooking odors.

One of the men cleared his throat. "Excuse me, Ma'am," he said. "My name's Jim Thornton, and this is my brother, Frank." They both had their hats off and were bowing politely.

"I am Mrs. Sullivan and this is my daughter, Nancy," Mama said.

"Howdy, Miss."

Nancy said hello. She liked these young men. They were polite, and looked like people you could trust.

The one who had said his name was Jim, obviously the leader, spoke again. "You traveling alone?"

"No," Mama told him. "There were four wagons in our party."

The young man hesitated. "I mean, your husband. He's —well—not with you?"

"I am a widow," Mama told him quietly. "My husband— my husband died on the way out."

"Oh, Ma'am, we're sure sorry."

There was an awkward silence for a moment. The young men looked at Mama, and then at each other. Mama, with Nancy helping her, continued with preparations for the meal.

Finally Frank spoke, perhaps thinking it was time to change the subject entirely. "I haven't smelled anything this good since I left home," he said.

That seemed to do it. Mama came to life, quick and sudden.

"Do stay and eat with us," she said. She sounded the way she used to when people came to the store and stayed until mealtime.

"We'd want to pay you," Jim told her, almost pleadingly. "I mean, it's just that we haven't had a home-cooked meal in months."

"Nonsense," Mama said. "I meant it when I invited you to be my guests. Bring a plate, Nancy. The ham's ready."

Mama began serving the plates. "If you don't mind sitting on the ground, the meal's ready," she told the young men. "Nancy, pour the coffee."

"Ma'am," they said, getting the words out all in a rush, both of them talking together, "We'd stand up to eat a meal like this, or maybe even stand on our heads." Each took a plate and a cup of coffee and went over to sit on the ground near the wagon.

"First decent meal we've had since we left home. Isn't it, Frank?"

And Frank said yes it was and took another bite of ham.

Mama put food on plates for herself and Nancy. Then they sat down on the wagon tongue and began to eat. It was almost like a party. The young men must have thought so too, for between bites they talked, telling their story. They had come around Cape Horn in a sailing vessel. Took months, it did, but finally they got here. Once they arrived, they started out to look for gold. Found some, too.

"We are both married," Jim said. "My wife and kids—we have two—stayed home, back in Kentucky. I want something to take to them. Frank doesn't have any children, but that doesn't keep him from wanting to find gold."

They were both eating nicely enough, but all the time giving the impression that, had they turned themselves loose, they would have gulped the food like starving animals. Mama looked over, saw their cups were empty.

"Give them more coffee, Nancy," she said.

They acted as if they didn't believe what they heard, but as soon as the coffee was in their cups, they were drinking it, not neglecting to thank her first.

"You just don't get a second cup of coffee when you eat in this town," Frank told Mama. "That is, unless you pay extra. That stuff costs money here. Big money."

Finally they were finished. They stood up and turned to Mama.

"Now Ma'am," Jim said, "I know you told us you wouldn't take any money. But would you accept a—well, a sort of gift?" Then, seeing Mama's hesitation, he went on quickly, "Just to show we enjoyed the meal, and all that. Honest, we really want to."

Mama, evidently realizing how sincere they were, said all right, she'd welcome the gift.

"We don't have any money, Ma'am, but we do have

some gold dust. They take that for money out here. 'Most anywhere you buy, they will."

Mama smiled. It was the first time Nancy had seen this happen since Papa's death.

"All right," she said. "That's what we started out here for, to find gold. Looks like we've already struck pay dirt."

Jim drew a small leather pouch from his pocket, handing it to Mama who said, "Thank you."

"Thank *you*, Ma'am," Jim said. He hesitated a moment, looked at Frank, and then turned to Mama again. "You meaning to stay here?" he asked.

Maybe it was his question. Maybe it was going through the familiar routine of preparing food and then having guests eat it with evident appreciation. Whatever the cause, something had happened to Mama. She was alive, alert. Almost the way she had looked when Papa was with them.

"If I could find a house," she said, no hesitation in her voice now, "I'd move in and serve meals."

"Serve meals . . ." The young men repeated the words after her. They looked at each other quickly. Perhaps they doubted her words, or didn't believe they had really heard her. "Serve meals?" Jim asked.

"Yes," Mama said. "But of course I'd need a house."

"They are mighty hard to come by," Frank told her. "Town's full of people looking for a place to live."

Jim shot a quick glance at his brother, as if to still further protest. Perhaps he was just being kind, not wanting to disappoint Mama after she had served them a good meal.

"Tell you what, Ma'am," he said, "we'll look around." He turned and started off in such a great hurry he almost tripped over his own feet. Frank was close behind him.

"Is it all right if we come back in the morning for breakfast and tell you whether we found anything?" Jim called over his shoulder.

"Come on," Mama told him. "At least I know I'll be here then." She made a joke of it, not acting as if she expected them.

They did come back in the morning, however, and they had news to report.

"We've found you a house," Jim announced. "The men who own it bought it before gold was discovered. Now they want to strike out for the Diggings and would like to trade their house for your wagon and team."

"Well," Mama said, "I don't need the wagon and team if I stay here."

"I reckon we ought to warn you, Ma'am," Frank told her. "It's pretty small." Then he added, as if it was something he should have thought of earlier, "Would you like to have a look before you decide?"

Mr. Morgan and Bill had been standing nearby, of course hearing the conversation, but saying nothing themselves. "What do you think?" Mama asked them. They joined the group and Mama introduced them.

Jim turned his attention to the men, probably feeling more comfortable discussing the matter with them. "We know the owners of this house," he said. "They do own it. They have the papers. We've seen them. They want a wagon and team so they can take off to look for gold. Better than walking, the way so many are doing."

Mr. Morgan nodded understandingly.

"Tell you what," Frank spoke up. "Why don't you people drive over and see for yourselves. Then if she likes it, she can stay." He nodded in Mama's direction, seeming very proud of himself for having thought of this.

"Good idea," Bill said. "We'll pack your things and get the teams."

Mama was silent a moment and then she said it was a good idea, but she wished Mrs. Morgan would go with them.

Finally they were ready and started off, the men walking ahead and Don with them. "I'm a big boy now," he told them proudly. The women were in the wagon. Mama was driving, taking the job over without hesitation.

"Here it is," Jim said, halting before a little box of a house sitting alone, vacant lots on both sides, and one across the street. At least we won't be bothered with neighbors, Nancy thought, half-tempted to giggle, but restraining herself.

Almost before they stopped, two men came out of the door. They wore red shirts and hats pushed back on their heads, and acted as if they were in a great hurry to be off and away.

"This is Mrs. Sullivan," Jim said, "the woman I was telling you about."

"You willing to trade?" one of them asked.

"We'll take a look," Mama told him. "Come on . . ." She motioned to Mrs. Morgan and Nancy. Houses were woman business.

They went inside, followed by the owners. The house was very small, as Jim had said. Three rooms, lined up like marching soldiers. The front one had a couple of chairs and a sort of counter; it looked as if it might have been used as a store at one time. The next one held a bed, a crude chest with a small mirror over it, and a couple of cots, all pushed so close together it was difficult to thread one's way around them. In the back room there was a stove, a table, four chairs, and a cupboard with an assortment of tin plates, cups, and knives and forks on the open shelves.

Nancy saw something near the back door that attracted her attention. A pump, complete with handle and spigot. Remembering her experience carrying water at the camp, she went over to it and pushed the handle up and down a few times. Water began to pour out the spout.

"Look, Mama," she said. "There's water." As far as she was concerned, that was enough to recommend the place to her. But Mama was evidently noticing other things as well.

"It looks fairly clean," she commented.

As indeed it did. Some of the floor boards and shelves

were still damp. Evidently the owners, either of their own accord or urged on by Jim and Frank, had undertaken a bout of housecleaning, thinking, perhaps, this would make a woman consider the place with more favor.

"Oh, yes," one of the men said. "And you have a pile of wood at the back door."

Mama opened the door and, sure enough, there was some wood. She nodded her head, closed the door, and then, followed by Nancy and Mrs. Morgan, went out to join Bill and Mr. Morgan, who looked at her questioningly.

"It will do, I guess," Mama said. "Seems fairly clean."

Mr. Morgan had others things in mind. "How about a title?" he asked. "A deed?"

"It's all right," Jim assured him. "We checked with a lawyer. We know one here. We talked with him last night after we found out the men wanted to sell the house. Just so we could be sure everything was all right."

They certainly were in a big hurry, Nancy was thinking. Was the same thought coming to Mama, too? That they were trusting complete strangers, accepting their word and their plan without question. Why would Jim and Frank be so anxious to help two women they had met only yesterday?

Then Nancy pushed the thought from her. Mr. Morgan and Bill were standing by. They could be trusted to help Mama make a wise decision.

The owners of the house began to shift restlessly from one foot to another. Plainly they couldn't wait to be off and away, looking for the gold which they felt sure was right around the turn in the road.

"Let's see that deed," Bill said to them.

"There'll have to be some other papers too." Mr. Morgan told them. "Something to the effect that Mrs. Sullivan is trading the wagon and ox teams for the house." He addressed himself directly to the men. "So if anyone questions your right to the outfit, you can prove it is yours. Mrs. Sullivan can sign as the owner and some of us as witnesses."

They wound up with an exchange of documents, the men handing over a legal-looking paper with a seal on it, and Mama a paper which she had signed, with Mr. Morgan and Bill, Jim and Frank as witnesses.

"Now," they said, almost as a chorus, "we'll unload."

They all worked at the unloading, even the former owners of the house—thinking, no doubt, that the sooner they had Mama's things out of the wagon, the quicker they themselves could leave.

"Put them down anywhere," Mama said. "Nancy and I will arrange them, once we decide where we want them."

When the last piece was out of the wagon, the two men drove off, not looking back. If Mama cast a single glance in their direction, Nancy didn't catch it. There were, evidently, no regrets on her part. With Don, it was different.

"Golly," he said, "I'm sorry you're staying here. I wish you were going on with us."

Mama looked quickly at Mrs. Morgan who walked over, arms outstretched.

"I hate to tell you, but—" She stopped, her eyes filled with tears. "We're leaving, too."

"Leaving?" Mama repeated, a question in her voice.

"Yes. You see, Bill knows this place, this spot where he says the mining is good. I don't want to, but Mr. Morgan—" she pointed in his direction—"is bound to go. I hate to take Don. I thought we could stay here in San Francisco and he could maybe go to school. But Mr. Morgan says there's not enough gold here, and I guess we have to go along with him."

"I understand," Mama said.

As of course she did. Hadn't she started out with Papa for the same reason, giving no thought about school for Nancy?

"What are you going to do?" Mrs. Morgan asked. "I mean, how will you get along? I feel terrible, leaving you here."

"Don't worry," Mama told her. "We'll manage."

"How?" Mrs. Morgan repeated.

Mama spoke up, clear and sure, her answer no surprise to Nancy. Why else had Jim and Frank found this house. "I'm going to serve meals," she said. "Nancy and I." She took Nancy's hand and as she did so, the girl was reminded of the other time Mama had reached toward her—the night after Papa died. "We can, can't we?" Mama asked, seeming to want reassurance.

"Of course we can," Nancy said quickly. "You've already started, really. With Jim and Frank."

"Well—" Mrs. Morgan hesitated, perhaps only half-convinced. "Anyway, I'll be thinking about you."

Mama said, "Thank you. You've been wonderful. I don't know how we could have done without you. If you ever come back this way . . ."

"Oh, yes," Mrs. Morgan told her.

The invitation was given and accepted, with both women probably thinking they'd never see each other again.

"Good-by—"

"Good-by—"

And the Morgans were gone, their wagon creaking off, with Bill following them.

"Ma'am." Nancy and Mama looked around and saw Jim and Frank standing there. "Ma'am," Jim said, "if we stayed and helped you get things in place, do you suppose you would be willing to feed us tonight?"

Mama considered the matter.

"I think so," she finally said. "Now let's go in and start." They went inside and set to work immediately.

"We'll put the two cots in the front room," Mama decided. "Use them for sofas."

They followed her directions. Nancy had her own ideas. She brought in the books and put them on the counter. Before long, the room did begin to take on the appearance of a living room. Of course, the middle room was a bedroom, and no mistake about it, and the kitchen was also a dining room.

"Looks real homelike," Frank said.

"Anything more you want us to do?" Jim asked.

"No," Mama told him. "Just come on back for supper."

"Oh, you can depend on that," they said, and left.

The meal was ready when Jim and Frank came back that evening.

"Smells mighty good," Frank said.

"Sit down," Mama told them.

They took their seats at the table. Jim cleared his throat. "We been talking to a few fellows," he said. "They wondered if you'd be willing to feed them too. I mean, you said you would serve meals, didn't you?"

"Indeed I did," Mama told him. "But if I do, I'll have to buy some groceries. I've pretty well used up my supply. Where shall I go for them?"

The young men both laid down their forks and looked at her.

"Well," Jim said, "you'll have to watch out. I've heard some places are charging a dollar apiece for eggs, and seventy-five cents for a loaf of bread."

"I make my own bread," Mama told him.

"I mean, that gives you an idea of the prices. But we know a place or two that stays open evenings. They won't exactly give you the stuff, but they won't take advantage of you either. Not with us there. Soon as we finish eating, we'll go with you."

"That's very kind of you," Mama told him, not protesting. She must have known she needed their help and guidance. A dollar apiece for eggs!

"All right," Jim said, when he had finished the last bit of food on his plate. "Let's go. Bring some baskets to carry the stuff back in." Then he hesitated. "You have some money?" he asked.

"Yes," Mama told him. "I—we—brought some from home. I have it in my reticule." She touched the bag in her hand.

"Good. But remember, gold dust, like we gave you, is worth sixteen dollars an ounce, and the shopkeepers will take it, same as money."

"I'll remember," Mama assured him. She found a couple of baskets, handed one to Nancy, and the four of them walked out the door of the little house.

Nancy looked around her. She could see tents and houses clinging to the summit of three hills, luminous, like lighted Christmas trees. Fog was coming in, so thick she could taste it. And yet it smelled and tasted clean and vigorous. The streets were unpaved and muddy. All sorts of people were making their way across them. Men from the United States, of course, and Chinese with long straight pigtails. And in great hats and sarapes, men Nancy supposed to be from Mexico or South America. A jargon of tongues filled the air. No way to tell where all the people had come from.

At a little distance to their left lay the town itself. A few taller, more sturdy buildings stood close together.

"Portsmouth Square," Jim explained. "The Plaza. Parker House is still the best hotel. Most of the others are just rooming houses. Post office over there too."

They did not go in that direction, however. Instead, they stopped at a store not too far from their house. When they walked in, a man was standing behind the counter. Nancy wondered if Mama was remembering, as she herself was, the store back home and Papa behind the counter, greeting customers.

"Mr. Fitzhugh," Jim said, "this is Mrs. Sullivan. She's a widow woman, and this is her daughter, Miss Nancy. They're cooking some mighty good meals for us. Treat 'em right." It was almost as if he dared the owner to do otherwise.

Mr. Fitzhugh looked at them closely, apparently liking what he saw. "Howdy, Ma'am," he said. "And Miss. What do you want?"

"Meal," Mama began.

"How much?" Jim broke in, looking at Mr. Fitzhugh.

The man swallowed hastily, and then quoted a price that was evidently fair enough, for Jim and Frank nodded together.

"I'll take ten pounds," Mama said.

That's the way the whole shopping expedition went. They made the rounds of several stores, getting prices before buying. Finally they had the things Mama seemed to think she needed most.

"I'm through," she told the boys. "We can go home now."

They walked with her, carrying the baskets containing the purchases. When they were back at the house, they went inside.

"We'll have some fellows here for breakfast," they told her. "That is, if it's all right with you."

"Of course," Mama said. "Bring them on."

They hesitated a moment, looked at each other, evidently trying to decide which one was to do the talking. Finally Frank broke the silence. "Mrs. Sullivan, Ma'am," he blurted out, "I reckon we ought to tell you. We're going to be off to the Diggings in a few days."

"Why of course," Mama said. "I had supposed you'd be going. Thank you for helping me so much."

"Good night," they said. "We'll be here with some fellows in the morning."

They settle us in the house, and then they leave, Nancy was thinking. They are going to send men to eat with us, but they themselves won't stay. And again, as she had done earlier, she pushed the doubts away. She and Mama had a roof over their heads, thanks to Jim and Frank. Mr. Morgan and Bill had examined the papers and had found them satisfactory. Certainly this was better than living in a wagon in the camp or trailing along after the Morgans and the others.

"It's time to go to bed," Mama said. "I want to have breakfast ready on time."

Nancy decided she'd concentrate on being grateful that Mama was more the way she used to be. The house, the promise of people coming for meals, had done that much for her.

Sure enough, early the next morning Jim and Frank were knocking at the door. With them were three other men, all young, all looking a little bashful.

"These are the fellows we were telling you about," Jim announced.

Mama greeted them cordially and told them to come in. Breakfast was almost ready.

"We noticed you didn't have many chairs," Frank told Mama, "so we found a couple of extras. Not very fancy, but we can sit on them."

He and Jim went outside and came back with two stools, crude but substantial. These they took for themselves, leaving the chairs already in the kitchen for the newcomers.

They sat down, acting as if just being allowed to watch Mama and Nancy prepare the meal was almost as good as eating it. Nancy set the table, being careful to have the cloth straight and the dishes properly placed.

"It's ready," Mama finally said, and began to dish up the food. Nancy carried it to the table, where the young men were already seated. She came back with the coffee pot and filled their cups.

"Thank you," they said. And then, as they took their first bite, "Ma'am, this is mighty good grub."

Nancy could feel the eyes of these newcomers following her as she moved about the kitchen. It was an entirely pleasant sensation, reminding her of the way she used to feel when Papa told her she was pretty. During those last trying weeks on the road she had given little thought to her appearance. Now, with these young men looking approvingly at her, it mattered once more. She decided she would wash her hair and unpack some of the dresses in her trunk. The pink striped cotton would be good. Pretty, but not too dressed up for working in the kitchen.

Jim and Frank stayed briefly after the others left. "It's like this, Mrs. Sullivan," Frank explained. "We just discouraged any people you might not want from coming."

Mama said she appreciated this. She meant to run a high class eating place, and that was the sort of people she wanted to feed.

For the most part, that was the sort who came. Even after Jim and Frank left for the Diggings, the group was pretty much the same. Young men, polite, plainly delighted with Mama's good food and reasonable prices. Usually they seemed to be new to town.

"Where you from?" they'd ask each other.

Iowa, maybe. Or Indiana. Or Virginia. They came from everywhere. They rarely stayed long, but pushed on to the hills beyond the Bay, sure they'd find gold waiting to be picked up with very little effort on their part.

Sometimes miners, coming back from hunting gold, paid with gold dust, as Jim and Frank had done. Mama had a box for this too. She guarded it carefully.

"Remember, Nancy," she said, "when our supply of salt gives out, I understand we could have to pay as much as three hundred dollars for a hundred-pound sack. If we are to continue serving meals, we must have money for more supplies, once these are gone."

Occasionally Mama and Nancy shopped for groceries, going in the daytime and usually buying from Mr. Fitzhugh. As they went, Nancy always looked toward the town, promising herself that as soon as she and Mama had some spare time they would explore a bit. Perhaps even go to the harbor filled with ships, their masts reaching up toward the sky.

"People come out here in anything that can hoist a sail or make steam," one of the young men said. "Most of those ships are just stuck there. Soon as ever they dock, the crew all rush off to the Diggings."

They might rush off, but the town was still filled with people, with the noise of wagons and carriages going over the muddy streets, with the sound of people talking in many languages.

One day a young man handed Nancy a package. "Buffalo meat," he explained. "For you and your Ma. It's right tasty. You ought to try it. A fellow came in with a lot of it and just sort of insisted I take some."

Nancy was sure Mama felt the same way she did about

these gifts. Partly they were for Mama, because the men were truly glad to come here for companionship as well as food. This was a touch of home most of them lacked now. But they were also a tribute to Nancy. So she always added her thanks to Mama's. And, also, she was careful about her own appearance, combing her hair carefully, donning the pink striped dress or the blue flowered one. Sometimes she even added a bow to her hair. She never failed to be rewarded with admiring glances.

"You sure do look pretty today," one of the men told her.

"What do you mean, today?" another one growled. "She always does look pretty."

Nancy could feel her cheeks getting pinker. She didn't really mind that she and Mama had to work most of the day, preparing the meals and cleaning up afterwards. In fact, they worked so hard that when night came they were glad to fall into bed. They would drop off to sleep almost immediately, scarcely hearing the sounds which filled the night.

One evening a very different type of man came. He swaggered in just before mealtime. "Name's Buck Frasier," he announced, his voice loud and a little thick. It was easy to tell he had been drinking. "Heard this was a good eating joint. I want something, and be quick about it."

Mama was busy at the stove, putting the last touches on the meal. Nancy noticed the others in the room were quietly waiting to be told when it was time to eat, not welcoming him as they usually did a newcomer.

"The meal will be ready before long," Nancy said. "Sit down, and we'll tell you."

Instead of taking a seat near the others, he pulled a chair up to the table, making a great noise as he did so. His clothes were dirty and unkempt; even his hands needed washing, Nancy noticed. She wanted to call his attention to the basin sitting on the stand by the pump, but hesitated to do so. Before long, Mama had the food on the table.

"It's ready," she said. Apparently she too had decided to ignore the man.

The others drew their chairs up and began eating. In contrast to them, the newcomer ate like an animal, gulping his food, making a great noise as he did so.

"Hey," he said, "more coffee." Not even a "please" out of him.

Nancy went over to refill his cup. As she did so, he made a grab for her. Instinctively she dodged back, in her haste tilting the coffee pot. A stream of boiling liquid hit him square on the outreaching hand.

He jumped up from the table, hurling a volley of oaths at her, words she had never really heard before, not even from the men in the wagon train they had joined on their way to California.

"I didn't mean," she began.

Without waiting for her to finish, he stormed out of the

room. The others were silent, watching him go. After the door slammed behind him, one of the men said, "You handled that real good. We were a little worried, when he came in." Evidently he was no stranger to them.

"But it was an accident," she said. "Honestly it was."

They acted as if they didn't really believe her but, at the same time, admired her for doing what she did.

"You'll get along all right," another one told her.

Gradually the house became more than just a place to eat. The boarders came early, visited with Mama and Nancy and with each other.

"I had hoped Nancy could go to school," Mama said one day as she was preparing a meal. Several young men sat in the kitchen, watching her.

"No use, Ma'am," one of them told her. "Soon as the Gold Fever hit, the schoolmaster lit out for the Diggings too."

Nancy said nothing, but secretly she wondered when she could have found time to go to school. She and Mama were forever either cooking meals or cleaning up after them or shopping for groceries. About all they saw of the town was this house and the route they took to buy necessary supplies. But they were making money enough to live on, and that was something they could be grateful for. Two lone women, making their own way.

One day a boy asked, "Ma'am, I got a buddy who'll be

coming in before long. Can I leave a note here for him?"
And Mama said yes, of course.

After that, it became a regular thing to do. Nancy was
the postmistress. She had a special shelf for the letters,
back of the counter in the front room. She would let no
one besides herself, except Mama, of course, come behind
the barrier. After all, that was the way a real post office
was managed.

One day a young man, a stranger to her, came in. He
glanced around, apparently to be sure no one else was
there. When he was satisfied they were alone, he said,
lowering his voice, "My name's Sam Kirby. I am—well.
I'm a friend of Jim and Frank. And of Zeke Fowler. We're
partners. Don't think you've met Zeke yet."

"No," Nancy told him. "I don't believe he's been here."

"He's out in the Diggings," Sam Kirby went on. "But
he'll be coming in here some of these days. I want to leave
this package for him."

He reached into his pocket and drew out a canvas bag
tied with leather thongs.

"You keep this real careful," he said. "I want Zeke to get
it. Nobody else." He put the package into Nancy's hand,
and then started out the door.

"Wait a minute," she asked, "how will I know him?"

"Oh, you'll know him. Reddest hair ever you did see.
He's tall, more than six feet. And he's got a voice like a
foghorn."

"Wait a minute," Nancy began. She wasn't at all sure

she wanted to be responsible for this package, whatever it was. But before she could finish her sentence, the man was gone. Nancy was still holding the package when Mama came into the room.

"A man just left this," Nancy told her. "He said he was a friend of Jim and Frank. He told me this was for their partner, Zeke Fowler. But he acted so . . . well, so strange, I wonder if I should have kept it."

"No need to think about that now," Mama told her sensibly. "You have it. Anyway, as I understand the matter, you really had no choice. The question is, what to do with it."

Which of course was right. Plainly it couldn't be left out here on the shelves, along with the other letters and messages. The man's whole attitude had indicated it was something very valuable.

"Here, let me feel it," Mama said.

Nancy handed it to her, conscious as she did so that the contents, whatever they might be, were quite heavy for so small a parcel. Mama took the bag. "Well," she said, "it's certainly got some weight to it."

They were both silent. Nancy knew Mama was thinking the same thing she was. Where would be a good place to keep it?

"How about under the mattress?" Nancy asked. "Then we could keep an eye on it day and night."

"Well," Mama mused, "I've heard that's the first place a prowler looks, but since most of the time we're either in the kitchen cooking or serving the meals, or in here passing out mail, or in bed, it might be all right."

Together they went into their bedroom, Nancy carrying the bag. Then, together, they raised the mattress, and stuck the package under it at the foot of the bed.

"Now all we have to do is to wait for Zeke," Nancy said.

They went out of the room. For the time being, the matter was dismissed.

It was nearly a week later when Mama said to Nancy, "I think I'll go down to the square. One of the boys told me I might be able to get some fresh buffalo meat there this afternoon. Without having to pay too much for it," she added quickly.

"Want me to go with you?" Nancy asked.

"No, not especially. I'd rather you'd pick over some beans and start them cooking."

"All right," Nancy said. She didn't have any real wish to see the meat on display. Never a pleasant sight, that.

"I won't be gone long," Mama told her, and walked out of the house, down the street toward the market. Nancy busied herself with looking over the beans, discarding any which seemed less than desirable. In the midst of her work, a knock sounded at the door.

"Come in," she called, not even getting up. Probably one of the men who ate there, stopping by to visit.

A man opened the door and walked in. He was short, maybe not more than five-and-a-half feet tall. He had dun-colored hair and pale blue eyes. Before Nancy could even speak to him, he said, "I've come for the package left here for Zeke Fowler." His voice was thin and high-pitched.

Zeke Fowler. Red hair. Tall. Voice like a foghorn.

"But you are not Zeke Fowler," Nancy told him. She stood up now, almost upsetting the pan of beans in her lap.

"I want the package," the man went on, as if he had not heard her.

"But I was told to give it to Zeke Fowler himself."

"Oh, that's all right. I'm supposed to take it to him."

You keep this real careful. I want him to get it. Nobody else. The words came back to her, clear as if the man who left the sack with her was standing at her side.

"I'm sorry," she said, "but I promised to give it to Zeke himself, and I must keep my word."

The man took a step toward her. Instinctively Nancy braced herself, thinking perhaps he would try to force her to hand over the package. Then he seemed to change his mind and walked toward the door. Just at the threshold he turned to look at her. After a moment of hesitation he went outside, closing the door behind him. Nancy had the strange feeling that she had not seen the last of him.

Before long Mama came back, a package in her arms. "Buffalo," she said, putting it down on the kitchen table.

"Mama," Nancy began, and then she told her all about the visitor.

Mama listened carefully, a thoughtful expression on her face. "You did right," she said. "You certainly should not have turned it over to someone who was obviously not the owner." She was silent a moment, and then went on, "I only hope Zeke comes soon. I don't want to be responsible for that package any longer than we have to."

Zeke Fowler did come a few days later. No question about his being the real one. Tall, red-haired, everything about him inspiring confidence. Only, his voice wasn't hoarse. Instead, it was weak. The voice of a sick man.

"I'm Zeke Fowler," he told them. And then he fell flat on the floor, right at their feet.

"Poor boy!" Mama cried. "Whatever is the matter?"

Zeke didn't answer. Instead, he began to mutter incoherently and finally stopped talking altogether. Mama lost no time.

"Let's get him to the bed here in our room," she said to Nancy. "He's very sick. You and I will use the cots in the living room."

This is the way they worked things out. Mama watched over the sick man day and night. Nancy helped during the day. Mama stopped serving meals. "It's best I don't have others around now," she explained.

The young men who had been eating with her seemed to understand. They too tried to help. One of them even brought a doctor. At least he said he was a doctor, but he didn't act as if he knew very much about medicine or anything else. He was nervous and uncertain and seemed to think that no matter what he said someone was going to dispute his word. He mumbled something that sounded like, "The fever." He left some medicine, and then disappeared and never came back.

"Left town," the young man who had brought him explained. "Think he was a quack anyway."

Mama sniffed the medicine doubtfully, and then pushed it to one side. She went to the kitchen and came back with a bottle of her own concoction, some she had brought out with her. Zeke was tossing restlessly back and forth on his bed. Mama spoke to him firmly.

"Here," she said, "take this."

He opened his mouth obediently and swallowed the dosage Mama had poured out for him. Once he had done this, he dropped off to sleep.

Mama nursed Zeke through his illness, dosing him with her own medicine the while. The combination worked, for finally he was better. Weak, but able to be up. And very grateful.

"You saved my life, Ma'am," he said to Mama.

"I was glad I could be of help," Mama assured him. "By the way, did you know you had a package here? Someone left it for you, weeks ago."

Zeke looked thoughtful. "Yes, Ma'am, I know it's here," he told her. He hesitated a moment. "But I want to give it to you."

"To me?" Mama asked. "Whatever for?"

"For saving my life," he said. "I'm going back to the

fields in a day or two. It's all because of you. But listen . . ." He stopped, looked as if he wanted to tell her something important, and then went on, "take good care of it. Hear me? And don't let anyone know you have it."

"You mean?" Mama asked uncertainly.

"One or two people may already know. Or, I think they do. But you be careful, hear me?"

Mama said she would. The next morning when she and Nancy awakened, Zeke was gone. He had slipped out so quietly, they had not heard him leave.

"We might as well open the package," Mama decided.

They did. There within the wrappings were some small round bits of shining metal. Together they looked at them in unbelief.

"Nuggets," they said, almost in a whisper. "Gold nuggets . . ." Real riches here. No doubt of that.

"We'll put it back where it was," Mama went on. "Under the mattress. When Jim and Frank come, we'll ask about a safer place."

Once they went to bed that night, Nancy found it difficult to go to sleep. It was almost as if she could feel the sack of nuggets pressing into her feet as she lay on the mattress under which the package was hidden. She wondered if she'd ever get accustomed to sleeping on it.

The next morning, however, she didn't even think about the nuggets. Mama was sick. So sick, in fact, she didn't get out of bed.

"I'll just stay here," she muttered, her voice scarcely above a whisper. "Feel so bad . . ."

Nancy did the best she could, bringing Mama water to drink, bathing her to lower the fever, trying, without success, to tempt her to eat, insisting that she take doses of her own medicine. Mama swallowed it without protest, but it didn't help her any.

The men who had eaten her good meals slipped in to see her, but she didn't seem to notice them. Which made them all know she was gravely ill.

"We tried to get a doctor," they said, "but we can't find one."

Then, almost as if she had wished them back, Jim and Frank came. "We hear your Ma's sick," Jim said. "Real sick."

"Yes," Nancy said.

"Caught the fever from Zeke, most likely," Frank went on. " 'Tain't right."

Nancy let that pass without comment although, actually, she was thinking much the same thing. Mama shouldn't have to pay such a high price for her kindness.

"We'll stick around," Jim told her. "We'll check often and we'll keep trying to get a doctor."

"Could we just look in on your Ma to say hello?" Frank asked.

"Of course," Nancy said.

They went into Mama's room, but she was asleep, lying quietly, showing no sign of pain or discomfort.

"We'll go," Jim said. "But we'll be back. You can depend on that."

Suddenly it seemed as if a great burden had rolled off Nancy's shoulders. She *could* depend on them; of that she was sure. For the first time since Mama had become ill, she felt some comfort and assurance. She went into the front room, leaving the door between it and Mama's room open. She stretched out on one of the cots, first pulling it close to the door so she could keep an eye on Mama, lying there in her bed.

She must have fallen asleep, for as if from a great distance, she heard Mama calling her.

"Nancy!"

Nancy was off the cot, into Mama's room, and at her bedside in what seemed like a single reflexive motion.

"Yes, Mama," she said. She knelt beside the bed, taking Mama's hand in her own.

"Such a good daughter," Mama whispered.

These were her last words. After that she was very quiet and when, a little later, Jim and Frank came in, they told Nancy, gently as they could, that Mama was dead.

Chapter 3

MAMA WAS gone and Nancy was alone, just as Mrs. Courtney had said. The fact of her aloneness came to her now as she stood looking around her in the little kitchen. Everything in the room made her think of Mama. The dishes, both the ones they had brought overland in the wagon and those left by the former owners. The cooking things. The food stored in cans and boxes. This was where Mama spent much of her time; it was almost impossible to think of the room without her.

Nancy still had on the clothes she had worn to the funeral service this morning. There had been no time to change before Mrs. Courtney descended upon her. No time to think, really. No one, except Jim and Frank, to turn to.

"Now listen," Jim had said before they left, "don't you be scared. We've found a tent. We plan to pitch it right across the street from you, in the vacant lot. We'll keep watch." They considered the matter, as if there was still more to say. "But anyway, you go ahead and lock your doors. Good and tight. You understand?"

"Yes," Nancy said. "I will."

"Wish there was a woman we could find to stay with you, but we just don't know one. Not right now, that is. We'll sort of look around, though."

She, too, felt the need for some woman to confide in, someone to talk to. But as Frank and Jim said, there wasn't anyone. Women were scarce in the town. Anyway, Nancy and Mama had been here such a short time, only a few months. That wasn't long enough to meet people, especially when they were busy cooking and serving meals most of the time.

Nancy sat very still now, resting her elbows on the kitchen table, cupping her chin in her hands. She had told Mrs. Courtney she would stay here. What she really meant, of course, was that she would not go home with the woman, no matter how much she insisted. But what of the future?

The fog that had hung over the town was gone; the sun was shining and the air was clean and bright. Maybe there was something about this crisp, fresh air that would help her clear up her problems.

"All right," she told herself, "let me think."

She had this house, small though it was. If she left it, strangers would probably take over without even asking permission. After all, there were hundreds of people mill-ing around looking for a place to stay. If she did decide to leave, she could more than likely sell it, with the demand so great.

As far as money went, though, she would have no real problem. There were the silver coins, the bills, and the gold dust paid to Mama for the meals. There were also the gold nuggets left by Zeke. Whatever she decided to do, she wouldn't have to worry about money.

She sat there a long time. Finally she stood up quickly, and as she did so, felt her knees grow weak and a strange gnawing sensation in her stomach. She tried to remember when she had last eaten. Morning, and now it was late afternoon. Little as she relished the idea of food, she supposed she had better cook something for herself.

She walked to the small stove and started a fire in it. Then she looked inside the cupboard to check the food on hand.

Mama had eaten almost nothing during those last days and Nancy had cooked little for herself. She saw some dried apples and a portion of a loaf of bread. She supposed she could make a meal out of them, and yet it might be better if she cooked something a little more nourishing. A few potatoes were left in the bin. A piece of ham lay on the shelf. She took them down, remembering as she did so that Mama was cooking these same things the evening Jim and Frank came by, the visit that had been the start of the life she and Mama had known in San Francisco. But she mustn't let herself think of that. Instead, she began preparing the meal, finding it good to be busy. She believed she would make some coffee too, although as a usual thing she didn't drink it.

Nancy busied herself with the cooking, realizing she had a great deal too much for one person, wondering, in fact, if she could manage to eat anything by herself. Even as she was thinking this, she heard a knock at the door. Opening it, she was not at all surprised to see Jim and Frank.

"Hello," Jim said, "we just kinda thought we ought to look in on you."

"Come in," Nancy urged. "Do come in. I was feeling very lonely."

They nodded, looking around the kitchen uncertainly. Plainly, they were missing Mama.

"She was a good woman," Jim said, shifting awkwardly from one foot to the other. "A mighty good woman." And then, "That coffee smells like your Ma's."

Nancy felt the words coming from her lips in a great rush. "If you'll eat what I have cooked," she said, "do stay for supper."

"Will we!"

They sat down at the table in a hurry, as if they thought maybe she might change her mind. She put the ham and the potatoes and fruit on the table. She poured coffee, and then they began to eat.

"And what are you planning to do?" Frank asked, between bites.

Then it hit her. Just like that. "I'm going to stay here and serve meals," she told them. Maybe she had known this all along. Perhaps that was partly why she could be so firm with Mrs. Courtney.

"Stay here. By yourself?" They laid down their forks and looked at her in unbelief.

"Yes."

"But you're . . . you're so young," Jim protested. He didn't sound a bit like Mrs. Courtney, although he was saying the same thing.

"I can cook. I helped Mama," she reminded him, ignoring the real nature of the protest.

"Oh, we know that," Jim told her. He acted as if he meant to say something else, but then changed his mind and went on, "One thing, you got two sure customers."

She said, "Thank you," and then told them to come back for breakfast. And they said they'd come back for a meal anytime.

"If there's anything we can do to help, let us know," Frank said. "Remember, we're just across the street."

She thanked them and said if she thought of anything she'd tell them in the morning, and then they left. Once they were gone, she washed the dishes and put the kitchen in order. This done, she went to bed. Now that she had made up her mind, she could sleep.

Sure enough, Frank and Jim were back for breakfast the next morning. They had another young man with them.

"Name's Carl Thorpe," they told Nancy. "Just got to town. We used to know him back in Kentucky."

"I'm glad you came," she said. "I promise to have a better meal tonight. Want to come?"

"We'll be here," they promised.

Once they had finished their meal, paid her, and left, she began a systematic checking of supplies. She would need to add some things to her stock. Meal for one thing. Potatoes too. There were beans left, but very little coffee. Tomorrow she'd go shopping for groceries.

This done, she decided she would set the rest of the house to rights. She began with Mama's things. There was a sadness in packing her clothes into boxes and putting them away. She had no place to store them, so she pushed the boxes under the bed. As she did so, she remembered the nuggets and much of the gold dust were under the mattress.

"They say that's the first place a thief would look," Mama had said.

Nancy turned back the mattress and stood there, thinking deeply. Then with a gesture that was almost automatic, she began removing the sacks. Where would be a safer spot?

She carried them to the kitchen and looked around her. Not with the dishes, nor with the cooking things. There they would be in plain sight of anyone who opened the door. She sized up the situation, and finally, on an impulse she could not quite analyze, she walked over to the cupboard where the supplies were stored. The bean keg caught her eye. Quick as thought, she opened it, dropped the sacks into it, and then raked the beans over them. Sure enough, there was no hint of their presence. Just a keg of beans on the kitchen floor, waiting to be cooked. She turned away, satisfied with what she had done. For the first time since Mama's death, she even giggled a little. Those beans had meant money in the shape of meals served. Why not let them take care of the money they had earned.

When the three men came for supper that evening, she had the beans heating on the back of the stove, the coffee pot beside them. Kraut was cooking, with some of the bacon fat and bits of bacon in it.

"Almost as good a cook as your Mama," Jim told her.

Frank and Carl grinned, looking sideways at her, plainly wondering how she would take this. She smiled back at them. Mama had been a good cook. And Nancy had helped her, learning as she did so. It wasn't always easy, but now she was glad she had the experience.

"How about breakfast?" Jim asked.

"Fine. Except I'll have to buy some groceries if I have anything to feed you."

"We'll go with you," Jim said.

"Oh, that won't be necessary," she told him. "After all, you showed . . ." She hesitated, then went on firmly. "You showed Mama and me where to shop."

"All the same, we'll go," Frank said. "Tonight. In the morning we'll be busy."

"All right. When you've finished, I'm ready."

It was dark when they came back to her house. She unlocked the front door and stepped in. Jim and Frank, carrying the basket, were following her. She lighted the lamp on the table, and then what she saw brought a scream to her lips.

"Look!"

The room was in utter chaos. Everything was pushed about, turned upside down, tossed on the floor. Quickly they made their way to the bedroom, finding it in the same condition. Yes, the mattress had been pulled off the bed. They went into the kitchen, discovered that it too had been ransacked. Food was pulled out of the shelves. Dishes thrown to the floor. She rushed across to the bean keg where she had hidden the nuggets and the gold dust. Either the prowler had not thought to look here or, what was more likely, had been surprised by their return.

"You locked the doors?" Jim asked.

"Of course," she told him. She pointed to the kitchen window. It was open, explaining the prowler's entrance.

"You keep your money here in the house?" Frank asked.

"Yes. Mama did. We didn't know any bank."

"And that stuff Zeke left you?"

"It's here, too."

The boys looked at each other, and then looked at her.

In that brief moment they seemed to have come to a decision.

"Tell you what," Jim said. "First we'll help you get this house back to rights."

They busied themselves putting the mattress on the bed, pushing chairs into place, replacing dresser and cupboard drawers. Nancy worked with them, and before long the little house was in reasonable order. Once this was done, they started toward the door.

"Now you go to bed," they told her. "Try to get some sleep. We'll take turns watching the place. Tomorrow we'll talk about what to do. Don't worry. We'll be outside. First, though, we'll nail all these windows shut." Which they did.

She tried to thank them, but the words tangled up in her throat. They seemed to understand anyway and went outside, closing the door behind them. She locked the door after them. Then she fell across her bed, fully clothed, and exhausted, she slept.

She was awake very early the next morning. For a moment she lay still, not understanding why she was wearing her dress and shoes instead of a nightgown. Then knowledge came to her and she stood up, feeling stiff and a little numb.

She walked to the kitchen. Once there, she drew water from the pump and washed her face and hands. She combed her hair and decided she would change her dress

as well; certainly the one she wore was wrinkled and anything but fresh. She felt better after this, more able to face
the day.

Outside the fog hung thick and heavy, as it so often did
in early morning. By noon the sun would probably be
shining brightly.

She built a fire in the small stove, set about cooking
breakfast. Before the coffee had even started to boil, a
knock came.

"It's us," Jim called. "You all right?"

She opened the door. "Come in," she said. "Breakfast
will be ready before long. Where's Carl?"

"He, well, he didn't come."

She started to ask if he didn't like her cooking, and then
she noticed that Jim and Frank both looked serious and
troubled.

"Did something happen to him?" she asked anxiously.
In this town, as everyone knew, tragedy walked open on
the streets.

"No, it's just that we needed to talk to you. Serious. By
ourselves."

"Yes," she said, her own concern mounting as she looked
at them. No light matter, this talking they meant to do.
"What's wrong?"

Jim started to speak, but she stopped him. "Wait. I'll
put the meal on, and then we can talk," she said.

None of them ate much, but over cups of coffee Jim and
Frank explained the situation to her.

"All right," Jim began, "I guess you might as well have the truth. Zeke Fowler is on the trail of something pretty big, and we are in on it."

This didn't surprise her, nor did she see any reason for concern on her part.

"That's why we've been in and out so much," Frank explained. "Scouting." He turned to Jim. "Aw, go on and tell her. . . ."

Jim hesitated, plainly searching for exactly the right words. If it's something he finds difficult to explain, it must be pretty bad, Nancy thought. She leaned forward to listen as he cleared his throat and then began.

"Well," Jim said, "there were four of us who had grown up together, back in Kentucky. Frank and I, Zeke and Sam. We were partners, like Sam told you when he left this package. Zeke came out here first."

"Then he sent word for us to come," Frank broke in.

"And by the time we got here," Jim went on, "he thought he had found some likely spots. So he sent us out to check them. If we found anything, we were to bring a bag of nuggets back and leave them for Zeke. Then he'd get us all together and we'd stake out our claim and start digging. We needed some sort of a place to meet, a central spot where we could leave messages. Safe."

"Yes," Nancy said.

The picture was beginning to come clear. Their concern about finding a place for Mama. The care they took to be sure she went to the right stores and was given the best prices. Seeing that only the right kind of men came for meals. She remembered thinking, when they first said they had found the house, that it had all worked out mighty fast. Then, later, because of their many kindnesses, she pushed the idea aside. Now it all came back to her.

"Then we just happened to come by the camp, and met you folks," Jim continued.

"Yes," Nancy said, knowing there was a coolness in her voice.

"We weren't planning to take advantage of your mother." Jim was begging Nancy to understand. "She said she wanted to find a place to live and serve meals. And we thought, what could be better. A nice, respectable widow woman with a daughter. Nobody would suspect you two. You wouldn't be doing anything wrong. Just doing good, serving those fine meals. We could leave our messages with you, and we knew it would be all right."

"Then," Frank broke in, "we got to liking her for her own sake. Your Ma was . . . well, a really fine woman, besides being a good cook. She, and you, made us feel at home. Men without a touch of home get to be . . ." His voice trailed off.

"Well, Sam did hit something that looked mighty good. He brought the nuggets to your place, so Zeke could get them, and know."

And we were left with the evidence, Nancy thought.

"Careful as we all were," Jim continued, "the word leaked out. We don't know how it happened, but somebody got the idea the nuggets were a map, telling the location of the strike."

Nancy was beginning to understand. "And they think I have the map?" she asked. "That's why the man was trying to get the package?"

"Yes. At least that's what we think. Not that the nuggets aren't valuable in themselves, for they are. But what that man—whoever he was—really wanted, was the map. He thinks it will give the location of the place where they were found."

"I understand," Nancy said. "At least, I think I do."

"We could talk till we turned blue in the face," Frank broke in, "saying you didn't have any map, that there isn't any map. But some people wouldn't believe us, would feel sure we were just covering up the truth."

"They think I have the map and they'll keep on trying to get it," Nancy said. "So it's not safe for me to stay here."

"Oh, I wouldn't say that," Jim hedged.

"But you think I should leave?"

"Well, yes. That's what it amounts to. Do you have anyone you can go to? A relative or a friend?"

If you ever need help. Papa's words came back to her, clear as if he were standing at her side.

"Yes, I have a cousin in New Orleans."

Cousin Matilda Hogan, whom she had never seen, whose last letter had been written more than a year ago. And failing her, who? The Collins, who had taken over the store? No. It must be Cousin Matilda. Her last letter was in the trunk with Mama's papers. Papa had always said she was kind and good, that if any of them needed help, they had only to get in touch with her.

"I have a cousin in New Orleans," she repeated, speaking as much to herself as to them. "Miss Matilda Hogan."

"All right, we'll try to figure out a way for you to go to her. A ship, probably."

"A ship?"

"Yes, just as soon as one sails. Harbor's full of abandoned ones," Jim said. "The minute they anchored here the crews joined the passengers and went off looking for gold."

"Some do make the return trip, though," Frank told her. "Guess it's so they can pick up another load to bring back. Lot of money in that deal. Ones going back aren't as crowded as those coming out. No trouble getting passage. Only thing, we don't know when one will be sailing."

"But we'll check," Jim promised.

Nancy was silent, considering the matter. She wasn't at all sure she wanted to give up so quickly and easily.

"Why can't I give those nuggets back to you, or to Zeke?" she asked. "We could spread the word that I don't have them any more. Then the person who wants them, or the map he thinks they are, would stop trying to take it from me."

"First of all," Jim explained, "that person, whoever he is, might not believe you didn't have it any more. Besides, we can't be sure the word would get through to the right one. No, it looks to us like the only thing for you to do is to leave."

They made it sound so simple, not seeming to think it was any problem for her to go around the Horn, sailing months to reach a cousin she had never seen. She couldn't write ahead about her coming, for she herself would probably arrive before the letter did. What would Cousin Matilda think of that? One did not make visits without first alerting the hostess. And then another difficulty occurred to her.

"This house. We bought it, you know," she reminded them. "I can't just walk off and leave it."

"Oh, there'll be plenty of people who'd buy it, hard as houses are to come by out here. We'll take care of that."

"All right," she finally said, still reluctant, but unable to think of any more objections. "Go ahead."

"We'll see about everything," Jim assured her, getting up from the table. "In the meanwhile, we'll keep watch on this place. But you be sure to lock your doors."

"I will," she told them.

And then they were gone.

The next day they came back, visibly pleased with themselves. They had found a buyer for the house. He'd also take the food and the furniture that was in it.

"He says he was a lawyer in Arkansas, where he came from," Jim explained. "But he didn't have a big practice, so he and his wife and kid, they lit out for California, hoping to find gold here. Traveled by boat, and they don't even have a wagon to stay in, like the people who came overland have."

"And he wants a place to leave the wife and kid while he's out looking for all that gold," Frank said. He grinned a little, probably thinking of how the man was in for disappointment.

Like we did, Nancy thought. Only Papa wasn't planning so much on the money as he was on the adventure.

"He wants to know, do you have a deed to this place. Being a lawyer, I guess he would think of that. The title those men gave your Ma when she traded, and those papers the three of them signed. Do you have them?"

"Yes," Nancy told him. She went to the little trunk and lifted the lid. In a way, the intruder had done her a favor. Because of him, she had found it necessary to put almost everything she owned back in place. Now she knew exactly where to look for the necessary papers.

"Here they are," she said, handing over the deed and papers.

"He'll probably want something saying you own the place," Jim told her. "Your Ma's name is signed to the papers, you know."

"What?"

"Oh, just something saying the place is yours, now that your Ma's gone."

"Here's a sheet of paper to write on," Jim said.

Nancy took the paper, looked thoughtfully at it a moment, and then wrote, "My mother is dead and I am her sole heir." She signed her name and handed it, together with the deed, to the young man.

"I think that ought to do it," Jim said. "We'll take it to him right now."

They started toward the door, but once there they stopped. "We don't think he's got too much money," Frank told her. "But if we can get enough out of him to pay your passage to New Orleans, would that be all right? Once you get there, you can cash in on your gold if you need money."

"I have some cash," she assured them. "Money from the boarders."

"That's fine. And by the way, we found out there's a ship leaving in a couple of days. The *Mary Pearl*. We've already talked to the Captain. He seems like a nice guy."

They haven't wasted any time, Nancy thought. As if they couldn't wait to get rid of me. Then she felt ashamed of herself for even letting such an idea come to her. Jim and Frank were looking after her own best interests. She could trust them. She *did* trust them.

"Thank you," she told them earnestly. "You are so very kind . . ." She couldn't go on, but she felt sure they understood.

Before long, they were back. They brought some papers

for her to sign. "Two of them," Jim told her. "One for you to give him, one for you to keep. They're identical."

"Just in case you want a record to prove you did turn this over to him," Frank explained.

Of course. That was the way they had handled things when Mama traded the teams and wagon for the house. She tried not to let herself think that marked the beginning of her life here, and this, the end. . . .

"It's just a form," Jim told her. "Read them and then sign. That is, if you want to," he finished.

He acts as if I have a choice, Nancy thought. She read the brief statement—something to the effect that she, Nancy Sullivan, was turning over all claim to her house. A description followed, giving location and other facts. She signed without question. After all, Frank and Jim wouldn't be doing this if it weren't all right.

"When we get the money from him, what do you say to having us pay your passage right away?" Jim asked.

"That's fine," she told him. It seemed now that she couldn't leave fast enough. Not only was there the threat of possible danger hanging over her, but, once she had signed the sale papers for the house, she had cut all ties with this place.

"We'll take these papers to the man," Jim said. "Then we'll get the ticket and bring it to you."

"Shouldn't take us long," Frank told her as they left.

Sure enough, it was only a short time before they were back.

"All worked out," Jim said. "Here's your ticket. The *Mary Pearl* leaves day after tomorrow."

"The Captain says there's a nice woman with a couple of kids who will be on the ship," Jim told her. "He's met her."

"We told him we'd appreciate it if he saw that you met her, and he said he'd do it. That way you'll have someone to sort of look after you," Frank said.

"Thank you," she told them warmly. "Oh, thank you for seeing to things. And now I must pack."

"We'll be here and see that you get on the ship," they assured her. "We'll bring some sort of a van, so we can take your baggage."

"You're taking so much trouble for my sake," she said.

"After all," Jim told her, "we got you into this."

Of course they had, but Nancy felt no bitterness toward them. Only a wish to reassure them. "You didn't mean to," she said.

"You're a real great girl," Jim said gratefully.

And Frank added, "Like your Ma."

They left, and Nancy went back to her packing. For the most part, it was a process of selection. Of course she could take neither the food left in the shelves nor Mama's cooking utensils. She hoped the woman who came to live in the house would appreciate them and use them well, as Mama had done. She decided she would take only what she could pack into the two small trunks, hers and Mama's, that they had brought out here in the wagon. Mama's clothes. Her own. There were not many of these. People traveling in covered wagons did not bring large wardrobes. Toilet articles. The few books. The sacks of gold dust the boys had occasionally used to pay for their meals?

The nuggets? No. These, she knew beyond any question, should not be in the trunks. Instead, they must be where she could keep her eyes on them at all times. Even though Frank and Jim felt it was the map rather than the nuggets the prowler was looking for, they were still valuable. They could well represent a major portion of her financial security in the months to come. At least she would not be going to Cousin Matilda empty handed, like a beggar.

She thought a long time. Then she got up with purpose in her movements. From Mama's sewing box she took a needle and thread and some pieces of strong cloth. With them she fashioned several small pouches. Once they were finished, she put the nuggets and the gold dust into them and sewed them shut. This done, she dropped them into Mama's reticule, which was large enough to hold them, but small enough for Nancy to carry.

It was a little like having Mama with her, for Mama had made the reticule herself, fashioning it from heavy, soft woolen material. She had embroidered around the opening through which the cord was drawn in order to pull the bag shut.

By the time Nancy finished the last of her preparations,

it was late. She laid out the clothes she would wear in the morning. She closed the trunk lids, turned the keys. As she did so, she felt that not only was it the trunks she was closing, but her life here as well.

Chapter 4

$\mathcal{N}$ANCY STOOD at the rail of the *Mary Pearl* as the ship moved out of the Bay, through the Golden Gate, into the ocean. Behind her was San Francisco and its sandy beaches, its hills rising sharply into the blue sky, and the small islands dotted with wooden shacks and miners' tents. In the Bay itself other ships were anchored, their masts looking bare and dejected. These abandoned ships had come out filled with people thinking only of rushing off to look for gold. They did not always find that gold, but even so, few of them sought passage back around the Horn to the eastern ports which they had left. Frank and Jim were right. The *Mary Pearl* had plenty of vacant space. Only a few people seemed to be boarding.

The two men stayed with Nancy until the last few moments before the ship sailed. They went with her in the small boat which rowed her out to the *Mary Pearl;* they helped her up the rope ladder she had to climb in order to board the ship; and once she was there, they took her to meet the Captain.

"Miss Nancy Sullivan," Jim said, being formal and polite, "meet Captain Dixon."

Nancy extended her hand and the Captain took it, saying, "Howdy do, Miss."

"You're to keep an eye on her," Frank reminded him. "Like we told you, she's traveling alone. Her mother is dead. Mighty fine woman."

"Yes," Captain Dixon said, "you mentioned that when you booked Miss Sullivan's passage." He didn't say whether they had told him about Nancy's being alone or Mama's goodness.

"I've assigned her a cabin on the top deck," the Captain went on. "Just across from Mrs. Porter and her children. Here's the key. Want to help her find it? Now if you'll just excuse me—" and he was off.

Jim and Frank carried her trunks to the cabin assigned her. It was indeed small. But just across from it was the door to the other cabin, the one Nancy assumed was occupied by "the woman with a couple of kids." Seeing it, she felt less alone.

"Well, I guess we better be going," Jim told her.

She shook hands with them, feeling tears come to her eyes. "You've been so very kind. Thanks, thanks for everything. . . ."

"Oh, we didn't do anything much," Frank said. "And

don't worry, he'll—" he pointed in the direction the Captain had gone—"he'll watch out for you."

She followed them to the ship's rail, waving good-by as they rowed back to shore. It seemed that only now she realized she was leaving. She stood there until she could no longer see Jim and Frank, her last links with San Francisco. She might as well go to her cabin. She walked back to it and went in.

Once inside, she unpacked, trying to decide what things she would need. It seemed strange to think that she would spend months on this voyage to New Orleans. What would she do to pass the time? Reread the books she had brought with her? Perhaps sew, making over Mama's dresses so that she herself could wear them? Her eyes fell on the reticule which held the nuggets. Should she leave them there? If she did, it would be necessary to keep her eye on it every minute, all during the long journey. It seemed much more sensible to store them in some safe place here in her cabin. But where?

Not under the mattress, certainly. She looked around the room. Her eyes fell on the small cupboard where her clothes were hanging. She made up her mind. Quickly she walked over and lifted the skirt to one of her dresses. Just at the waistline she attached the pouches containing the nuggets and gold dust, making them secure, using a needle and thread from Mama's sewing kit. Then she dropped the skirt and stood back to take a careful look. No hint that anything was hidden in it.

At that moment a knock came at her door. When she opened it, Captain Dixon stood outside.

"I thought I'd see if you were getting along all right," he explained. Evidently he was remembering he had been told to look after her. "And take you to meet this lady who is just across from you."

"Thank you," Nancy said, and stepped outside.

"Name's Porter," he said, knocking at the woman's door.

"Yes?" a woman's voice answered.

"Captain Dixon, Ma'am," he told her. "There's someone here I'd like you to meet."

Mrs. Porter opened the door and came into the corridor. Nancy liked her on sight. A kind and gentle person, but with a quality of determination about her.

"This is Nancy Sullivan, Mrs. Porter," the Captain said. "She's traveling alone. Her mother's dead. She's going to a cousin in New Orleans. She has the cabin just across from you." He gestured toward Nancy's door.

"Why honey," Mrs. Porter said warmly. "It's good to meet you. Do come to me if you need anything. Promise."

"Indeed I will," Nancy assured her. "And thank you."

"Why don't you eat with us," Mrs. Porter suggested.

"I'd like that," Nancy said.

"I'll knock on your door when we are ready to go down," Mrs. Porter told her. "It shouldn't be long now?" She looked inquiringly at Captain Dixon.

" 'Bout half an hour," he said. "And now I must be

going." He was off again, to look after whatever duties were his.

"Half an hour then?" Mrs. Porter said.

And Nancy said yes, she'd be ready. She went to her own small cabin. She smoothed her hair, washed her hands, checked to see that her dress was hanging straight and even. She wanted to look exactly right when she was with Mrs. Porter.

It wasn't long before the knock came and Nancy stepped outside, closing the door behind her. There stood Mrs. Porter with the two children.

"This is Betty," she said, indicating a little brown-eyed girl with a look of shyness about her. "She's ten."

" "Hello," Betty said softly.

"Hello," Nancy said.

"And this is Mark," Mrs. Porter went on.

"I'm eight," he declared proudly, indicating he thought that was the best of all ages. Nothing shy about him.

"Oh, hello," Nancy said again. She was remembering Don Morgan and thinking it was good to have children around once more.

"Let's go down to the dining room," Mrs. Porter suggested, and the three of them—Nancy, Betty, and Mark—followed as she led the way.

There was no one in the dining room except a waiter, who bowed politely and led them to a table. Once they were seated, he bowed again.

"Thank you," Mrs. Porter said.

"*Sí*," he answered, bowing even more deeply.

Sí. That was Spanish for "yes." This boy probably spoke no English at all. Nancy searched her mind, trying to recall some of the phrases she had learned when she and Papa chattered together.

"*Habla español?*" she asked.

The boy's face lighted up with pure delight. "*Sí, señorita. Mi nombre es Pacho.*" He burst into a torrent of words, ones Nancy knew to be Spanish, although she could understand only a few of them.

"*Hablo español un poco,*" she told him and then, turning to Mrs. Porter, "I told him I spoke Spanish only a little. My father taught me what I know. This boy says his name is Pacho."

By now he was gone, but before long he was back with their food, serving them with great care, plainly anxious to have everything exactly right. Apparently there was no menu in this ship's dining room. You chose from what was set before you, the way the boarders did at Mama's table.

"It looks as if we are sure of one friend aboard," Mrs. Porter said, smiling at Nancy. "Thanks to you."

Thanks to Papa, Nancy thought. He taught me these few words I know.

"I have another son," Mrs. Porter said, once they were eating their meal. "Rex. He's nineteen. He's with my husband in Panama."

Nancy was wondering what they were doing in Panama when the rest of the family was here on the *Mary Pearl*, but she was too polite to say so. Mrs. Porter must have guessed her thoughts.

"They've gone ahead to make arrangements for our trip across the Isthmus," the woman explained. Again, she sensed Nancy's question.

"We're going back to our farm in Missouri," she said. "It's lots quicker that way. Takes months to go around the Horn or across by land, the way we went out."

"We went overland, too," Nancy told her, remembering Papa, the old sadness returning. She felt Mrs. Porter's question.

"My father died on the trip," she explained simply.

Mrs. Porter reached out to pat her hand. "You poor darling," she said, her words warm and comforting. Then she went on to talk of other things, knowing Nancy would have it so.

"We'll take the boat from New Orleans, go up the Mississippi to St. Louis, and be back home in time to put the crops in."

"I'm going to New Orleans, too," Nancy told her.

"Yes, I know. Captain Dixon said you were. Too bad we'll be gone long before this boat gets there."

"Oh, yes . . ." Nancy's voice broke off in a note of surprise so great that Mrs. Porter turned to follow her gaze and see what was wrong.

Mrs. Courtney was walking into the dining room. She looked around and then, seeing Nancy and the Porters, hurried to their table.

"Why hello," she said, acting as if she had known Nancy all her life, the way she had done when she had come to the house the day of Mama's funeral. "So you're on this ship, too. Where are you headed for?"

Nancy had the feeling, strange but nonetheless real, that Mrs. Courtney knew quite well where she was going. She really didn't act at all surprised.

"New Orleans," Nancy said. And then, quickly, to shut off further questions, "I'm going to a cousin who lives there."

"Is that so? It just happens we are going to New Orleans too. My husband isn't well. I'm taking his meals to him."

"Oh," Nancy said. And then. "This is my friend—" She was telling the truth, really. Mrs. Porter *was* her friend, of that she was sure. "This is my friend, Mrs. Porter, and her children, Betty and Mark."

They all spoke, but Nancy could see Mrs. Courtney was eyeing Mrs. Porter thoughtfully. It seemed very natural for Nancy to continue, "They're going to New Orleans too."

Mrs. Courtney said, "Oh . . ." and then went over to a table and sat there alone. When Pacho came to her she began to talk rapidly to him. He stood looking at her helplessly and finally went out of the room. Presently he was back, bringing someone with him. Evidently it was the cook, for he was wearing his apron tied securely around his fat middle.

"What you want, lady?" Nancy heard him ask.

"My husband is ill," Mrs. Courtney told him. "I want to take his meals to him."

"Oh, all right," the cook said. "I'll bring you something."

When Pacho served her meal, he brought another plate covered with a napkin. He set them both down before her, bowing as he had done when he served Nancy and the Porters.

"I'll bring the plate back," Mrs. Courtney promised. Pacho bowed again, although, more than likely, he didn't in the least understand her.

"Your friend," Mrs. Porter said, a note of reserve in her voice. "Hadn't you known she would be on this ship?"

Nancy could read the woman's thoughts. Captain Dixon had said Nancy was alone, and here Mrs. Courtney pops up, acting like a lifelong friend.

"I've seen her only once before," Nancy explained quickly. "She came to my house the day my mother was buried."

"Oh . . ." Mrs. Porter said.

"She insisted that I go home and stay with her," Nancy went on, feeling the need to tell exactly what had happened. "I didn't know her. I didn't want to go. And I didn't," she finished.

Something about her words, her way of speaking, seemed to satisfy Mrs. Porter. "I think you did right," she said, and leaned over to pat Nancy's hand.

Mrs. Courtney ate quickly, paying no attention to the other passengers who were now beginning to come into the dining room. All men, Nancy noticed. They looked vague and quiet. Probably they had given up finding the gold they had gone out to look for, and now were going back feeling defeated and discouraged.

Mrs. Courtney finished and left, carrying the plate of food meant for her husband. As she passed the table where Nancy sat, she nodded brightly.

Nancy and the Porters took their time, sitting at the table talking. Finally they got up and started toward the door. Pacho rushed ahead to open it for them.

"*Gracias*," Nancy said, and then turned to Betty and Mark. "That's Spanish for 'thank you,' " she told them.

"*Gracias*," they said together, obviously much pleased with themselves.

Pacho beamed and bowed deeply.

Outside the door, they saw Mrs. Courtney talking earnestly with Captain Dixon who was shaking his head vigorously. She walked away just before Nancy and the Porters came to where the Captain was standing.

"That woman," he said. He seemed anxious to talk to somebody, and since they were handy, chose them. "She's running me crazy."

Nancy wanted to ask why, but hesitated to do so.

"Wanting to change their cabin," he went on. "Says their place is most unsatisfactory. No fresh air. Makes her husband sick. Wants to be up where you and Mrs. Porter are."

"Oh," Nancy said, unable to think of any other reply.

"And I told her she couldn't be choosy, coming in at the last minute."

"After I did?" Nancy asked curiously, remembering her own reservation had been only two days before the ship sailed.

"After you did. I should say so. Matter of fact, she and her husband came down early this morning, not long before we sailed. Seemed in a great rush to get on. Said they had an unexpected message to come to New Orleans right away, and they must take this ship. Late as they came, they were lucky to get on."

Of course he was exaggerating. The ship wasn't really crowded at all. It must be Mrs. Courtney's highhanded ways, not the shortage of room, which was bothering him. Nancy could understand his irritation. She herself had felt the same way the first time she had seen the woman. Once more she was grateful for having the Porters. She didn't want to let herself think about how Mrs. Courtney would have tried to take over, had Nancy been traveling alone.

She was increasingly grateful as the days went by. Not only did she eat with the Porters, she was with them much of her waking hours. When Betty and Mark saw her coming, they left their mother and rushed toward her. When they wanted to go walking around the deck, it was Nancy who went with them more often than not. Together they watched the waves piling high against the ship. They saw the fish jump out of the water and then land back into the waves. Pacho gave the children table scraps which they threw to the gulls and other sea birds that often followed the ship.

The children also struck up a friendship with Pacho. They even began picking up Spanish words so they could carry on a conversation of sorts. When they saw him they always cried, *"Buenos días."* Mark explained that it meant hello, sort of. Pacho said it did. They called beans *"frijoles."* Nancy found herself speaking Spanish, adding new words to her vocabulary, increasing her understanding of the ones she had learned from Papa. All the time Pacho was beaming on them, helping them in their mastery of the language.

"We're getting real smart," Mark bragged.

One day Nancy woke to find the skies outside leaden and gray. Soon after breakfast the rain came, sloshing across the deck, making any kind of outside activity impossible. The children stood looking disconsolately at the rain.

"What will we do?" they asked, turning to Nancy.

The girl had been wondering about that too; not for their sakes, but for her own. Suddenly inspiration came to her. "You come into my cabin with me," she suggested. "I have some books we'll read. Go ask your mother if it's all right."

"Oh, goody," they said together and were off in a great rush to get the necessary permission. Nancy wasn't sure whether they were really interested in reading or just wanted something to do.

Inside her cabin she began selecting books, handling them gently. They were a touch of home, of her own childhood. Papa had read to her from them. They had gone to California in the wagon with her. From some of them she had read to Don, using them as the basis for his lessons. Now they would help Mark and Betty pass a rainy day on board the ship.

"Here we are," she heard Mark calling outside her door, and she opened it to let them in. "Mama says it's fine."

"Sit down," she told them. "Here are the books." She handed one to each child and kept one for herself.

The children were genuinely interested. They read aloud to each other, with Nancy listening. They read by themselves, sitting quietly, forgetful of the rain outside. Before they knew it, the morning was gone and it was time for lunch.

"Can we come back?" they begged. "Oh, please, can we come back?"

"Of course," Nancy assured them.

"It's like school," they told her. "Only more fun."

And then Betty added wistfully, "We haven't been to school for such a long time."

An idea came to Nancy. "How would you like to come in every morning for a—" She hesitated, wanting to put the matter before them in exactly the right way—"for a sort of play school?" Again she was remembering Don, and was grateful for the experience she had in helping him. "We'd have reading and writing, and maybe a few sums."

"Oh, would we!" they cried together.

That was the way Nancy started her school. Two students, both of them anxious and eager for the experience. In good weather they met in a protected spot on deck. At such times Pacho often joined them, standing in the background, listening carefully. Occasionally Mark or even Betty, forgetting her shyness, would address a few words to him, sometimes in Spanish, more often in English. He seemed to be understanding more and more of their language, as they were growing in their ability to understand his. Occasionally Mrs. Courtney would pass by, looking sour and discontented, obviously wanting to break in on the lesson, but not quite daring to do so.

"At least I can be thankful for that," Nancy told herself.

If it was raining, the children came to Nancy's cabin. They read. They did a few sums. They wrote a theme now and then.

"You don't know what this means to me," Mrs. Porter told Nancy. "I've been concerned because the children weren't in school. I should have been teaching them myself, I suppose, but I must confess I was tired. The trip to California, the whole experience there wasn't easy."

"I know," Nancy assured her.

It hadn't been easy for Mama and Nancy either, or for those others who went with them. It probably wasn't easy for anyone making the trip overland. Some of them found gold, but to others the trip brought nothing but disappointment, or even worse. She wondered about the Porters. As if reading her thoughts, Mrs. Porter said, "Ned, my husband, thought he'd go out and find a fortune, just like that. We lived on a farm in Missouri. Farming isn't easy work, you know. Of course gold mining wasn't easy, either."

She was silent, perhaps thinking over those days in California. "He found some gold. Not a fortune, but some. And he decided he'd buy the farm we had been renting. It belonged to his family, and he wanted to buy out his brothers and sisters. They didn't want to farm. They have other interests. One is a merchant. Another teaches school."

She was silent again for a moment, looking out at the ocean. "Now," she said, "we have enough money to do what we want."

Nancy found herself feeling very glad for the Porters; it was as if their good fortune was her own also. She and Mrs. Porter sat talking on deck until finally the woman said, "My goodness, I didn't realize how late it was. Get to bed in a hurry. And don't bother about classes in the morning. If you have them at all, they can come in the afternoon."

Nancy, with no classes to think about, slept late. When she looked at her watch and saw what time it was, she first thought she would not eat breakfast at all. She finally decided to dress hurriedly and rush down. If it was too late, at least she would have tried.

When she came to the dining room, Pacho was nowhere in sight, but the cook said she could have some coffee and a piece of bread. She took them and settled herself at a table. Of course the Porters were already gone. So was everyone else. The cook was just being kind to her, letting her have something this late.

She thanked him and started back to her cabin. As she walked along, she saw another cabin door open. Mrs. Courtney came out, carrying a plate, the one on which she had taken breakfast to her sick husband, no doubt. She left the door open and walked away in the opposite direction from Nancy, evidently not seeing her.

Nancy walked on. She was almost even with the door out of which Mrs. Courtney had come, when she saw a man in the room, his back turned to her. The sick husband, she supposed. He was walking about briskly, not acting the least bit sick. He turned, started toward the open door of the cabin. Nancy ducked into a corridor so she would be hidden from him. If he was pretending to be sick, there was no point in letting him know she had seen him.

He came to the cabin door and stopped there, looking in both directions, up and down the hall, furtive and watchful. Nancy, out of his sight in the corridor, regarded him curiously. Why all this secrecy? Was he hiding from someone he thought might harm him? Then he turned so that, although he still could not see her, she had a full view of his face. She stood there, not wanting to believe what she saw.

It was the man who had come to claim Zeke's nuggets. No mistake about it. The pale eyes, the sandy hair, the short stature. She could never forget him or mistake him for someone else. His face was fixed firmly in her memory. Just at that moment the sound of footsteps sounded in the hall, and he ducked back into his cabin, closing the door behind him.

So that's Mrs. Courtney's husband, Nancy thought wildly. He's hiding in their cabin, and he's not any more sick than I am!

Chapter 5

Nancy went inside her cabin and locked the door. She could not quite explain why she did this; certainly she was in no danger in broad daylight with people walking about on deck. Even so, she was frightened and, she felt sure, not without reason.

Mr. Courtney was the man who had tried to get Zeke's nuggets, not for the nuggets themselves, valuable though they were, but rather because he thought the bag contained a map giving the location of the rich lode Zeke and his friends had discovered. And now he and Mrs. Courtney were on the boat with her, bound for New Orleans as she was. She began sorting out the sequence of events, piecing them together as one would a puzzle, and the answer she got did nothing to allay her fears.

Mrs. Courtney, appearing at the house almost as soon as Nancy was home from Mama's funeral service. Acting as if she were a lifelong acquaintance, insisting Nancy go home with her. The ransacking of the house the first time Nancy left it after Mama's death. The Courtneys' request that their cabin be moved so they could be closer to Nancy, a request which Captain Dixon—for reasons he never bothered to explain—had not seen fit to grant. And the most terrifying fact of all, Mr. Courtney hiding in their cabin, pretending to be sick. Why? Did he plan to stay there during the entire voyage? Was he hiding, as Nancy suspected, because he thought she might recognize him? Or—and she tried to push the thought from her, with little success—was he waiting until Mrs. Porter left when the ship docked at Panama City? With her gone, Nancy would be without any real friend. Captain Dixon? No. He was far too busy to take on added responsibility. Besides, if she did try to tell him, he would probably think she was just a silly girl imagining things. Who else? Other people were on the boat, but Nancy scarcely knew them. She had been so happy in her friendship with the Porters she did not need to look to others for companionship.

Mrs. Porter. She would talk with her. Nancy got up quickly and started to the door. Once there, however, she stopped. What would she say? That the Courtneys were trying to steal a map they thought she had, a map which did not exist, never had existed? Could she make the story sound convincing? Was there any basis for her suspicion that Mrs. Courtney was trying to cultivate her friendship in order to get her hands on the map? Or that the Courtneys were on the *Mary Pearl* because of her? Or that Mr.

Courtney had some sinister reason for pretending to be ill and staying out of sight?

She considered the matter for a long time. By and by another thought came to her. Even if all her suspicions were true, would it be fair to involve Mrs. Porter? To do so might result in having the Courtneys include her in their plot, if such there was. No, Nancy knew she must handle this herself.

Her room became a prison she could endure no longer. She unlocked her door and went outside, being careful to lock it behind her. Scarcely was she on deck when Betty and Mark came racing to meet her.

"Where have you been?" Mark asked accusingly. "We've looked everywhere for you."

Nancy reached out a hand to each of them, and together they began walking around the deck. Something about the children's welcome, their very presence, helped her. Already she felt better, a little more confident.

"We wanted to tell you that we get to Panama City tomorrow," Mark went on. "Captain Dixon said so. And guess what. Pacho is going there, too."

"He says *'soy de Panamá'* or something like that," Betty explained, looking proud of herself. "That means 'My home is Panama.' At least I think it does."

"Of course," Mark told her loftily. "Golly, I wish he'd go across the Isthmus with us, clear to New Orleans. Wouldn't that be fun? I mean, having him along so we could talk to the people we meet. I bet they all speak Spanish, too."

The children probably were right about Pacho's living in Panama. They understood enough Spanish now to get the gist of a conversation. For one fleeting moment Nancy felt even deeper concern. Pacho had been someone she could count on but now he too would be gone.

Betty looked up at Nancy, her brown eyes anxious and troubled.

"I wish you were going with us," she said. "What will we do for our lessons?" Then, obviously thinking she had said it all wrong, she went on quickly, "Oh, we like you anyway, even if we didn't have any lessons with you. You're nice. Besides that, you're real pretty."

Nancy squeezed the child's hand so hard it surely must have hurt her. Betty had just given her an answer. Well, maybe an answer to her problem.

"If you'll excuse me," Nancy told the children, "I need to go to my cabin awhile."

They said that was all right, but Nancy scarcely heard them. A few moments ago she had felt she could not bear to stay in the cabin another minute. Now she couldn't wait to get back.

She let herself in and closed the door. This time she did not bother to lock it. Instead of being afraid, she was completely occupied with the idea that had come to her. Why couldn't she ask Mrs. Porter for permission to join them in their trip across the Isthmus? What excuse would she give for not going around the Horn as she had planned? The very logical one that by going with them she would reach New Orleans much sooner. Why spend months on a trip that could be made in a few weeks? No need to mention the Courtneys at all.

She wouldn't make any trouble for the Porters. After all, she and Mama had come overland in the wagon, part of the way without Papa to help them. She was accustomed to meeting the difficulties a trip might offer. She could ride horseback, if that was the way to go; she could walk if necessary. Back in Illinois she had often ridden; on the trip west, she had walked many times just for the sake of being out of the wagon. And if the children really wanted lessons, these could continue during the trip.

Best of all, she would be free of the Courtneys. Once the Porters were gone, Mr. Courtney wouldn't stay in his cabin all the time, as he was doing now. Of this Nancy felt sure. Every waking minute she would be afraid of what might happen with him roaming about the deck; as far as that went, she wouldn't feel safe at night either, even with her door locked. Now that the prospect of relief was in sight, she could see how difficult things would be if she remained on the *Mary Pearl*.

Her mind was made up. She opened her door, went outside, and knocked at Mrs. Porter's cabin. "It's me, Nancy," she called.

"Come in," Mrs. Porter said, opening her door.

Nancy stepped inside, and suddenly everything seemed

safe and right. "Mrs. Porter," she said, "I'd—I'd like to ask you something."

"Yes, of course."

Mrs. Porter had been folding clothes, evidently packing so they could leave the ship when it came to Panama City. She stopped her work, looked at Nancy. "What is it?" she asked, her tone implying that the request was already as good as granted.

"Could I . . . would you let me join you when you leave the ship tomorrow?"

"But I thought . . ." Mrs. Porter looked at her keenly now, evidently surprised.

"I was going around the Horn. Yes, that was what I had planned. But now I have decided I'd rather go across the Isthmus, with you. If," she added hastily, "you'll let me."

Nancy's voice trailed off. Maybe this wasn't such a good idea after all. She could feel Mrs. Porter's question; even, perhaps, her doubt as to the reason back of the decision.

"It's faster," Nancy explained simply. Which, of course, was the truth. "I can be in New Orleans weeks before this boat will arrive." Again, she spoke the truth.

Something about Nancy's explanation must have convinced Mrs. Porter, if, indeed, she had any real doubts to begin with.

"Why honey," she said warmly, "of course you can go with us. We'd love to have you. But I think you should know the trip will not be an easy one. Even with Papa and Rex making the necessary arrangements, we'll probably run into difficulties."

She paused a moment, and then went on, apparently thinking Nancy should know the nature of these difficulties. "I understand we ride mules part of the way and go in crude boats down a river some of the time. We have native guides, and they have been known to desert passengers, and make way with the baggage. I've heard all sorts of stories. . . ." Her voice trailed off.

"I know it won't be easy," Nancy said. "But I'll be with you, which is the important thing."

"And it will be good to have you," Mrs. Porter assured her. "I know the children will be pleased."

"As a matter of fact, they have already asked me," Nancy told her.

"I guess they thought that settled matters," Mrs. Porter laughed. "The way you've spoiled them . . ."

Nancy scarcely heard her, for another thought had come to her. What would the Courtneys do if she left the ship at Panama City? Would they decide to get off, too, and follow her across the Isthmus, making a great nuisance out of themselves? Perhaps even a downright threat? Would they think she had never meant to go around the Horn to New Orleans as she had told them she was doing? She could see all sorts of possible difficulties for herself, and perhaps even for the Porters, if she carried out her plans.

"Mrs. Porter," she said, "I believe I'll not mention my going with you. Just walk off when you do."

Mrs. Porter looked at her keenly. Perhaps she did suspect something.

"You'll have to tell Captain Dixon," she said. "Otherwise, he'll think maybe you've fallen overboard or were the victim of foul play."

"I'll tell him," Nancy agreed. "But no one else."

"You may be sure I won't mention it," Mrs. Porter said. She didn't sound offended, just understanding.

Nancy went out of the door, back to her own cabin. Now that the matter was settled, she felt a great relief. Tomorrow when the *Mary Pearl* docked at Panama City, she'd leave with Mrs. Porter and the children. In the meanwhile, she must tell Captain Dixon of her decision, giving as her reason the fact that she would arrive sooner in New Orleans. Then she would pack her trunks so as to be ready when the time came.

She waited until she saw the Captain alone on deck and made her way to him.

"Captain Dixon," she said, "I'm planning to leave the ship at Panama City when it docks tomorrow."

"But . . ." He looked at her uncertainly. "You asked for passage around the Horn, to New Orleans."

"I know," she said simply. "I've changed my mind."

"You've paid your passage."

He was an honest man and genuinely concerned. Even

so, she couldn't tell him the real reason for her decision. Perhaps she was wrong, after all. And yet something stronger than a mere hunch made her feel she was doing the right thing. Even so, she owed him an explanation.

"I'm going across the Isthmus with the Porters," she told him. "It takes less time, I understand."

"Well, that it does," he admitted. "But don't expect it to be easy. The things people tell about going across that little strip of land. Robbers, and varmints, and fever." He added to Mrs. Porter's list.

"I can stand it."

"If you insist," Captain Dixon said, "I guess there's no stopping you. But I am going to refund the unused portion of your passage money. After all, you're not a fourth of the way there by ship."

"I know," Nancy told him. "But it's not your fault."

"If you'll excuse me," he said, "I'll get the money."

He was gone only a few moments. When he came back he handed her some bills. "What I estimate to be the price of the rest of the trip," he explained. "Now put them in a safe place."

"I will," Nancy promised. She hesitated, and then went on with something she felt was necessary to say. "I don't plan to tell anyone but Mrs. Porter and you."

He looked at her searchingly, but before he could ask the question she knew was in his mind, she said quickly, "And thank you, thanks for everything you've done."

"Oh, that's all right." His voice was a bit gruff; Nancy

couldn't tell whether he was pleased with her thanks or questioning her decision.

She walked off, leaving him shaking his head. He probably suspected she wasn't telling the whole truth. She couldn't be bothered about that, however. If she were to leave with the Porters in the morning there was much to be done. Her trunks had to be packed, her clothes put in order. The nuggets and gold dust must be taken out of the woolen skirt where she had sewed them and put into Mama's reticule, which she would carry with her.

Once she was back in the cabin, she began packing with purpose and a feeling of assurance that things were going to work out fine.

She awoke very early the next morning. At first she was conscious only of the feeling that something nice was going to happen. Then she remembered and jumped out of bed. She dressed carefully, and once this was done, went across to Mrs. Porter's cabin and knocked. Betty opened the door; she too was dressed, as were Mark and Mrs. Porter. Behind them were the trunks, closed and waiting to be carried off the ship.

"You are ready?" Mrs. Porter asked.

"Yes," Nancy told her. "My trunks are packed." She paused for a moment, and then went on, "Could I have mine taken off with yours? I mean, as if they were a part of your baggage."

"Of course," Mrs. Porter said. "As a matter of fact, I was going to suggest that myself."

She knows there is something back of all this, Nancy thought. Some day I'll tell her everything.

"We'll need someone to carry them for us," Mrs. Porter said.

"I'll get someone," Nancy promised.

"Good. I'll leave that to you."

Nancy went outside, knowing exactly what she meant to do. She would find Pacho, if possible, and ask him to look after the baggage. She located him without difficulty. Seeing her, he bowed deeply. *"Buenos días,"* he said. "Good morning."

"Pacho," she began quickly, "listen . . ."

Partly in Spanish, partly in English, she told him. She was getting off the boat at Panama City with the Porters.

"Bueno," he said. "Nice peoples. *Muy."* He was obviously proud of the English he knew, even though he frequently lapsed into Spanish.

"Would you . . . would you take my trunks—*baúl*—to Mrs. Porter?" She gestured in the direction of the Porter cabin. Then, clearly as she could, speaking slowly, going into her knowledge of Spanish when he looked puzzled, she made him understand. He was to take her trunks off with the Porter baggage. But there was more than that to the job. When she had finished, he said, *"Sí,* yes," and she felt sure he grasped what she was saying—that no one except Captain Dixon and the Porters and, of course, Pacho himself, knew she was leaving the ship.

"I go at the last minute," she said.

"*Sí.* Yes, *Señorita.*"

He followed her to her cabin. Once there, he picked up her trunks, one at a time, and transferred them to Mrs. Porter's cabin.

"Oh," Mrs. Porter said. "You did find someone."

"Yes," Pacho told her. "I . . ." He gestured toward the trunks. And Nancy knew, as she was sure Mrs. Porter did also, they need have no further concern about the baggage. It would be taken safely off the ship and they would find it once they were on land.

There was a feeling of excitement on board the *Mary Pearl* as the ship drew near Panama City. Nancy saw the red tiled roofs rising bright against the sky, with a background of palm trees and greenery above and around them.

"Can't get any closer than two miles," Captain Dixon explained. "Harbor's full of silt." He answered Mrs. Porter's questioning look. "You'll go in by small boats, the same way you got to the ship in San Francisco."

This time I won't have Jim and Frank, Nancy thought. But I'll have Mrs. Porter.

Pacho came by, and Nancy could see he was carrying one of her trunks. Of course, he'd go back for the other one. No need to worry about that. She clutched the reticule tightly. In it were pouches of gold dust and also the precious nuggets, the little pieces of gold which she felt had been responsible for most of her troubles.

Even as she watched, she saw Pacho coming back. In a few minutes he passed her, this time with her second trunk. He continued making his trips back and forth, and now Nancy recognized the trunks she had seen in Mrs. Porter's cabin. These were larger than Nancy's and more difficult to handle. But he managed, by a dint of pushing and pulling, to get them to the ship's rail beside her baggage. When they were there, he stood close by, keeping watch. He did not so much as look in her direction; oh, he knew quite well there was some reason to proceed with caution. Nancy waited until Mrs. Porter, accompanied by Betty and Mark, had made her way to the rail. Then she followed them. At the side of the ship she could see small wooden tubs, fastened securely.

"You get into them," Captain Dixon explained. "They'll let you down into the boats that will take you to shore."

Mrs. Porter and the children climbed into one. As Nancy clambered over the rail into her tub, she looked around instinctively, half-expecting to see the Courtneys ready to leave too. But no. They were doubtless in their cabin, thinking they could relax now. Once the ship took off from Panama City, the Porters would not be with Nancy all the time.

The boats were waiting for them, the men who were to row them yelling across the water. Spanish, Nancy knew, although she could catch only a word now and then because they were all talking at once, and very fast. Since there were so few leaving the ship—the Porters, Nancy, and Pacho—the men on the small boats were all trying to get the passengers for themselves. Mrs. Porter looked with uncertainty at them. Nancy heard a voice speaking firmly, and with purpose. It was Pacho.

He gave instructions quickly, with authority. Then he motioned to one boat, indicating that Mrs. Porter and the children and Nancy were to use it. The owner nodded quietly; he evidently understood what was expected of him.

Pacho himself got into a second boat, taking with him some of the baggage. He chose still another boat to carry the rest of it. For a moment Mrs. Porter looked concerned. Leaving her baggage with someone else, even Pacho, who had been more than kind? The boy seemed to understand her thoughts.

"I see you." He pointed to the shore. "*Pronto—*"

"See you, Pacho," Betty and Mark called together. "*Muy pronto.* Very soon . . ."

It was not too long before they were at the wharf which was crowded with people—all sizes, ages, and, apparently, nationalities.

"Going back to San Francisco?" a man called out. "I mean, that ship out there?" He pointed to the *Mary Pearl.*

"No," Mrs. Porter told him. "To New Orleans, and then to New York."

The man groaned. "We been waiting here weeks," he said, "expecting a ship to take us on."

Mrs. Porter did not answer him, for suddenly two men had stepped to the front of the crowd and were waving wildly.

"There they are!" she cried. "Papa and Rex . . ." She was out of the boat almost before it had stopped, the children close behind her. Nancy alighted more slowly, keeping her eyes and ears open. The two men were moving toward the Porters.

"Papa!" Mrs. Porter cried, throwing herself into the older man's arms. "You're thin."

"Just a touch of the fever. Nothing much."

Before he could finish, Betty and Mark were both hugging him at once and Mrs. Porter had turned to the younger man.

"Rex," she said, burying her head on his shoulder.

The boy was tall, with brown eyes like Betty's, and hair verging on red. Strong looking; dependable. He's older than I thought he'd be, Nancy decided. She stood in the background, a witness to the reunion. Strange, she did not feel really left out, even though, as far as the Porters were concerned, she might as well have been in another land.

Mrs. Porter must have sensed that, for she turned and reached a hand toward the girl. "Nancy," she said, "my husband, and my son, Rex."

They both said hello.

"Nancy Sullivan," Mrs. Porter added. "And she wants to

go across the Isthmus with us. She's headed for New Orleans."

"Oh," Mr. Porter and Rex said together, neither welcome nor unwelcome in their voices. Merely surprise.

"She was on the ship with me," Mrs. Porter explained. "I don't see how I could have managed without her."

"And she taught us our lessons," Mark and Betty chimed in.

Mr. Porter and Rex both smiled now, warm and welcoming. Then they looked beyond Nancy and Mrs. Porter to where Pacho stood waiting, the various pieces of baggage around him.

It was Mark who took over the introductions. "This is Pacho," he explained. "He taught us Spanish. Didn't you, Pacho?"

"*Sí.*" Then he pointed to the men standing near, the ones who had rowed them from the boat.

"*Dinero,*" he said, gesturing toward them. "Money."

"Oh, of course."

The men broke into a torrent of Spanish once more. Pacho shook his head at them, and they looked disappointed but not rebellious. He named a price, and Mr. Porter reached into his pocket. Then Pacho turned to Nancy, indicating what the charge would be for her trunks. She opened her reticule and brought out the amount mentioned.

"And this," she said, "is for you. Oh, thank you, Pacho."

Even though he shook his head, unwilling to take the

bills, she insisted. Mr. Porter, seeing her gesture, brought some change out of his pocket.

"Thank you for helping my family," he said.

Pacho seemed to understand the spirit, if not the words. He bowed again and said, "*Gracias*—thank you."

Nancy reached out to take his hand. "We thank you," she told him. "Now, good-by. Good luck."

"*Adiós*," Betty and Mark said together. Pacho stepped back into the crowd.

"I'm in Panama City," Nancy told herself. "Before long I'll be starting across the Isthmus with the Porters." For the first time since the idea had come to her, she could let herself believe it would really happen.

Chapter 6

THEY STOOD on the wharf, their trunks at their feet.

"Guess we better get them to our rooms," Mr. Porter said. "It's not too far." But he looked uncertainly at the baggage, plainly not sure how to carry it. Because of me, Nancy thought, there are two extra pieces.

Almost before Mr. Porter had finished speaking, a dozen or more native boys rushed toward him, grabbing at the trunks, plainly meaning to carry them away, with or without permission. They were gesturing and talking at the tops of their voices, all speaking so fast in what sounded like Spanish, although Nancy, with her limited knowledge of the language, could not understand what they were saying. Their meaning was clear enough, however. They were going to carry the trunks and they had no intention of doing this as a courtesy to the new arrivals. They were to be paid, and well.

Rex and Mr. Porter seemed to be trying to decide which

ones to choose from the group, and Nancy found herself wishing for Pacho, who could manage this as he had done at the landing. Then, as if she had wished him into existence, he stepped forward. He pointed to himself, to the money they had paid him, and then in his mixture of Spanish and a few English words, explained that he was supposed to see that their baggage was taken to their rooms.

Nancy translated this message to Mr. Porter who, obviously much relieved, said yes, of course. "Tell him so," he said.

Nancy made Pacho understand he was to select the bearers. He turned to the group hovering over the trunks and spoke rapidly in Spanish. At his words, all but half a dozen or so stepped back once more into the crowd.

"*Dónde?*" Pacho asked. "Where?"

"Come," Mr. Porter said, and led the way. "It's where we've been staying," he told Mrs. Porter.

With the help of Pacho and Rex, the boys who were selected picked up the trunks and followed Mr. Porter. Mrs. Porter and the children and Nancy were at the end of the procession. Nancy thought perhaps the woman wanted to be sure those trunks really did go in the direction her husband had indicated.

They left the wharf, passing into a street so narrow no vehicle of any kind could travel over it. On both sides were two-story houses, most of them made of brightly painted wood. The sidewalk itself, only a few feet wide, was crowded with people. Chinese wearing pigtails Nancy recognized. Others she knew must have come from the four corners of the world. Compared to Panama City, San Francisco had been a small, quiet American village.

Soon they came to a wider street filled with drays and wagons pulled by oxen. Pack trains of loaded mules plodded along. All of them were headed toward the wharf. Nancy remembered Jim and Frank had said everyone was going to San Francisco, not away from it. Everyone except the Porters and me, she thought.

"Here we are," Mr. Porter said, stopping in front of a drab, rather uninteresting building. "We have a couple of rooms here."

"Not very fancy," Rex told his mother, evidently preparing her for what she would find when they were inside. "But we'll be here only one night. They're not too expensive. For rooms in this town, that is."

Nancy knew what he was trying to tell them. The same thing had happened in San Francisco. The ones who rented rooms charged just about any price they cared to name.

"Lots of people sleep outside," Mr. Porter said. "On benches. Even in the streets. The town is running over with people. Most of them waiting for a ship to San Francisco, but some are here working on the railroad. You know, the one across the Isthmus."

Of course they knew. Once that was finished, everyone said going to California would be easy.

They went inside the rooming house.

"Good afternoon," the owner greeted them, speaking English with no accent at all.

"Here we are," Rex said. "My mother, and sister and brother, as we told you." He stopped, turning toward Nancy. "And a friend," he added.

Nancy gave him a grateful look. It was good to feel she was accepted as a friend, not someone who had more or less thrust herself upon the family.

"I gave them the room next to yours, the way you asked me to," the proprietor told him. "Here's the key. Just go on up."

Rex and Mr. Porter led the way down a hall, the trunk bearers following them. They came to a door and stopped. Mr. Porter unlocked it and stood back for the others to enter.

Two narrow cots were pushed against the wall. In one corner were some hooks, evidently meant to serve as a wardrobe. On a small, rough stand stood a jug of water and a battered tin basin. That was the extent of the furniture. Through an open door they could see the adjoining room which was identical, except here there were three cots.

"Your room," Mr. Porter told Mrs. Porter. "You and the . . ."

He stopped in mid-sentence, but Nancy knew what he was going to say. This room was for Mrs. Porter, Betty and Mark. An awkward silence fell over the group. It was

Mark who solved the situation, probably without even knowing one existed.

"I'm sleeping in the room with Papa and Rex," he said. "I'm not going to stay with the women." Then, evidently being aware of the two cots, he continued, "I'll sleep on the floor."

They laughed then, and Rex reached out to tweak his ear. "All right, big boy," he said, "you can stay with the men."

They were conscious of the trunk bearers now, standing behind them, impatient and eager to be paid so they could leave.

"In there," Mr. Porter told them, pointing to Mrs. Porter's room. They carried the trunks to the designated spot and then stood still, waiting to be paid.

"How much?" Mr. Porter asked, and Nancy passed the question on to Pacho, although, of course, he knew what it was before she told him.

"*Dinero*," Pacho said, pointing to each trunk.

"A dollar each," Nancy said.

Mr. Porter reached into his pocket for the money. Nancy, before any question could come up, drew two dollars from her reticule, handed them to Pacho, who passed them along with Mr. Porter's money to the men who had carried the trunks. They didn't look too happy over the amount, but seemed to realize that, with Pacho in charge, nothing could be done.

"They've been setting their own prices for everything

they do," Rex said. "I guess it's hard for them to be reasonable."

All the bearers left, with Pacho at the end of the line. As he started out of the room, Mark reached to take his hand. "Stay awhile, Pacho. Teach me a little more Spanish before you leave."

Pacho understood enough to know the spirit of the request, if not the exact meaning. He stepped to one side with Mark and the two of them began a spirited conversation, their usual mixture of English and Spanish and many gestures. Nancy felt Pacho was not simply humoring a small boy. Actually, he seemed reluctant to leave these friends he had made on the trip from San Francisco, and welcomed a chance to stay awhile.

"Better start getting things organized," Mr. Porter said. "We leave early in the morning. Already have the guides and the mules engaged. That was part of the plan we worked out." He hesitated, and then looked at Nancy. "But . . ." he said.

Plain as if he had said the words, she knew the nature of his question. "You don't have a mule for me," she said.

"We didn't know you were coming," he told her, and then looked as if he wished he could take the words back.

It was the truth he told, Nancy realized. Of course they had no idea an extra person would be in their party. She felt embarrassment, concern, regret. It had been most inconsiderate to invite herself to go with them. How much she had taken for granted. How little she had known about the real situation. Only a very stupid, or selfish, or ignorant person could have done what she did. She trusted the family would lay it to ignorance.

"Listen," she began. "I . . ." She was going to tell them she did not have to go with them, all the time realizing what it would mean if she stayed here in Panama City where she knew no one, had no place to go. Better for her to have remained on the *Mary Pearl,* facing whatever might have happened. Surely, with Captain Dixon's help, she could have managed the Courtney problem.

Mrs. Porter, who must have sensed what she was thinking, reached over to take Nancy's hand.

"After all you did to help me," she said. "After the way the children turn to you. No, we can find some way to take you with us." She turned to Mr. Porter. "Can't we?" she asked, sounding a little uncertain now that she had made the promise.

"You don't have to feel responsible for me," Nancy told her earnestly.

She could feel Rex looking at her, his brown eyes clear and level. A man's look on a boy's face. She was glad, for no reason she could name, that she had dressed carefully before getting off the ship, that her hair was in order, with the ringlets framing her face.

"I think we can manage to find another mule," he said evenly.

Nancy felt a quick flush coming to her cheeks. Here was acceptance, even approval.

Across the room Mark and Pacho were still engaged in an animated conversation. "*Mañana*," Mark said. Pacho said, "*Sí, sí.*" It would be difficult to say who was enjoying himself most.

And then the idea came to Nancy. "Pacho," she cried.

"*Sí, Señorita?*"

"Listen . . ."

She told him, using the combination of Spanish and English they always employed in their conversations, that it was necessary for her to have a mule if she were to go with the Porters. He nodded as she talked, indicating he understood.

"*Sí.* Yes. Can get. *Mañana.*"

"Early," she told him.

"*Sí.* Tonight I find." He was out of the door, almost before he finished speaking.

"He'll be back," Nancy said confidently.

"Yes," Betty spoke up. "Pacho always does what he says he will."

Mrs. Porter turned to the trunks sitting on the floor. "Well, he helped bring the trunks here. For awhile I was afraid we'd never see them again."

Nancy saw Mr. Porter and Rex exchanging glances. Each seemed to say to the other, "You do it." Finally it was Rex who spoke.

"Mama, I hate to tell you," he said, "you can't take all that stuff across with you."

"What do you mean?" Mrs. Porter asked.

Rex gestured, a helpless movement, and turned to his father. "You tell her," he said.

"We must travel light," Mr. Porter explained. "We couldn't carry those trunks to Cruces on mule back. From Cruces we go by small boats. No room for trunks there, either."

"We need to move fast," Rex took up the explanation. "This is the dry season, now in February. If we fool around we could be caught in the rains." He spread out his hands to indicate the magnitude of this problem.

"Besides," Mr. Porter continued, "it's hard to watch baggage you don't carry with you. We heard that sometimes native carriers desert you in mid-passage, for no good reason. Others may walk off with the trunks and you never see them again. You can't be sure exactly how much money they'll demand. Sometimes it's a form of blackmail, we're told."

"Which means we should take only as much as we can carry with us on the mule we ride, and on the boat," Rex said.

"You mean . . ." Mrs. Porter began.

Just then a bell began clanging in the front of the hotel. "It's time to eat," Mr. Porter explained. "When we finish we can come back here and start the repacking."

"Don't expect anything fancy," Rex warned them as they made their way to the dining room.

Certainly, as Rex had warned them, the food was plain

and far from elegant. A bowl of rice, some beans, a platter of fish, another of fat pork.

"I've eaten so much pork I'll probably start grunting before long," Mark said. "We had it on the ship just about every meal."

"I hate to tell you," Rex warned him. "You'll see more of it while we're going across the Isthmus."

A bowl of fruit—bananas, pineapples, coconuts, and others unfamiliar to Nancy—sat in the middle of the table. Mark and Betty both reached for a portion.

"No," Mr. Porter told them. "Not here."

Native fruits, he went on to explain, often made newcomers ill. "Have to watch out for fever," he said. "And sick stomach. Remember, it won't be too long now. Only about sixty miles across the Isthmus and we'll be headed for New Orleans. Then, up the Mississippi, and pretty soon we'll be home." He made it sound like no trip at all.

"It can't be too soon for me," Mrs. Porter said.

Mr. Porter smiled indulgently at her. He seemed to understand exactly how she felt. He probably was as anxious as she was to be back home.

"What if we miss the boat to New Orleans?" Mrs. Porter asked.

"There's more than one," Rex told her. "The mail boats run three or four times a week. Now, as soon as we're finished, let's go to our rooms and start packing."

"I'm ready," Mrs. Porter said, and they made their way back to their rooms.

"Take only what we can carry ourselves," Nancy was

thinking. How could she select from those two trunks, hers and Mama's, what to take?

When they were back in their rooms, Mrs. Porter and Nancy unlocked their trunks and began looking at the things inside.

"What should I take?" Mrs. Porter said, talking more to herself than to anyone else. Nancy, regarding her own trunks, was thinking the same thing.

Mr. Porter and Rex came into the room, dragging some canvas containers. "Saddlebags," Rex said to Mrs. Porter. "For the things you want to take with you. We'll put them on the mules we ride. Yours and ours."

"Not the guides'," Rex told her. "Although we feel we can trust them. I hired them through some Americans, sort of agents, who live here. Even so." He shrugged his shoulders.

Then he looked uncertainly at Nancy. "We'll either get you a saddlebag, or you can share Mama's," he said.

"No," Nancy said quickly. "That won't be necessary."

"What will you do? You must take some things with you."

"I'll find a way."

And she would. She began taking articles out of Mama's trunk, thinking that possibly these would be among the first to be discarded.

"Incidentally," Mr. Porter said, "I suppose it isn't necessary to tell you that you won't need winter clothes as you go across."

Nancy was folding one of Mama's dresses. A warm,

woolen one made of strong homespun material. It had been right for the cool, foggy weather of San Francisco, but on the trip across the Isthmus it would be of no use at all. Or even in New Orleans, once Nancy was there. An idea came to her.

"I have my saddlebag," she told Mr. Porter. Then, at his questioning look, she said, "Here," and held out the dress. "I can sew it up at the bottom," she explained, "and then, once it's packed, fasten it shut and pull the waist over like a lid."

"Good girl," Mr. Porter told her approvingly. He turned to Rex who was watching quietly. "She's got a head on her shoulders," Mr. Porter finished. And Rex grinned and said, yes, he guessed she did.

"Now wouldn't she look funny without a head," Mark said. Everyone laughed, and after that the problem of selection went better. Not easy, but better.

Nancy decided to make three stacks on the cot. One, things she knew beyond a doubt she must have, mostly her own clothes with only a few items belonging to Mama. The other, ones she knew she could leave. And in between, some she couldn't quite make up her mind about just at the moment.

Certainly toilet articles would go with her. And her own lighter-weight dresses. Books? They would be on the doubtful pile. As she took them from her trunk, her hand touched something smooth and cool. The medicine bottles. She had not thought of them since leaving San Francisco.

Seeing them, she remembered Zeke and Mama's illness. She stood still, looking at the bottles. Only a few left now. Most of them had been used during Zeke's and later Mama's illness.

Mr. Porter would not allow the children to eat the fruit on the dinner table, saying there was a danger of fever and sick stomach. He himself had the fever while he and Rex waited for the family to come. Mama's medicine had helped Zeke, even though it did not save her own life. It was not an infallible cure, but there was no use discarding anything that might be useful. Without further hesitation, she placed the bottles on the stack of things she would take.

The packing was almost finished. Nancy was folding a soft shawl that had been Mama's, thinking she would put it on top of the improvised saddlebag. If, by any chance, a cool night came during the trip, she would have a wrap handy. Just then Mark came in to announce that Pacho was back.

"I told you he would come," the boy reminded them. Nancy looked up from her packing, and there Pacho stood.

"I come," he said. "I find mule and *muchacho*—boy—to lead."

They all went into Mr. Porter's and Rex's room, while Pacho, with Nancy to act as interpreter, explained. He had a friend whose brother took people across the trail on mules. The friend would go to Cruces now because many people were waiting there to be brought back to Panama

City. He would furnish the extra mule and go with the Porters.

"How much?" Rex asked.

Pacho held up ten fingers. "*Dinero* . . ."

"Fair enough," Rex said. "Some of them ask, and get, sixteen dollars or more."

"We leave early in the morning," he told Pacho. Then he turned to Nancy. "You tell him," he said.

But Pacho understood. "*Sí. Mañana.*"

"*Gracias,* Pacho," Mark said. "*Gracias mucho.*"

"*Muchacho bueno,*" Pacho said, grinning at Mark and patting him on the head.

"He says I'm a good boy," Mark announced proudly. "Only, it comes out 'boy good.' They say boy first."

"Oh, yes, Pacho, thank you very much," Nancy told him, thinking they had found many occasions to be grateful to him recently.

He started out of the room, and Nancy turned back to her packing. As she did so, her eyes fell on the pile of clothes to be left behind.

"Wait, Pacho," she cried, "Wait . . ." He stopped, probably thinking she had need of more help.

"Listen," she began. "*Su madre*—your mother. These clothes."

She pointed to the pile lying on the cot, the ones she felt she could not take with her. Then she went on, trying to explain that these things must stay here, together with the trunks they had been in. Would his mother like to have them?

At first he looked as if he could not believe he understood. Then he began to nod vigorously, and say, "Sí—yes. *Gracias* . . ."

Mrs. Porter turned quickly, her face bright. "And these," she pointed to her piles of discarded articles. "You take? Maybe a brother? Sister?"

Pacho looked puzzled, so she pointed, first to Betty, then to Mark. Pacho understood then. "Sí. Yes. So . . ." he gestured, measuring a height slightly less than Mark's, and then to Betty, indicating one about the same as hers.

"You take," Mrs. Porter said, her hands turned palms upward, in a giving gesture.

Pacho seemed almost overcome with the kindness. He kept saying thank you in Spanish and in English.

"You might as well stay here until we have finished," Mrs. Porter told him. "Then you can take the trunks with you."

Nancy made him understand that as well.

Packing became a little easier now. They worked so fast, there was no time for feeling sorry about what must be left.

"Actually it isn't too hard leaving these things," Mrs. Porter said, folding a well-worn dress. "We didn't take many really good clothes along. If we found gold, we could buy new ones; if we didn't, we could go back home." She spoke softly, obviously not wanting Mr. Porter to hear her.

"And the children grow so fast," she continued, "most of these are too small for them now."

She looked across at Nancy. "I have so much more room than you do," she said. "Maybe I could find a place."

Nancy wouldn't even let her finish the offer. "You also have more need for space," she said.

"You are a mighty fine girl, Nancy," Mrs. Porter told her. "Remember, we are glad you are going with us."

Something warm and happy flooded Nancy's heart, rushing up to her throat, blocking the "Thank you" she wanted to say. It really wasn't necessary to speak, however. She knew Mrs. Porter understood.

Before long the packing was finished, with the things that could be left behind put into the trunks. Nancy turned to Pacho, who had been waiting in the other room.

"Ready," she told him.

He walked outside the rooming house, stood at the door, and spoke a few quick sentences. Almost immediately some boys appeared. His own friends, most likely. In a rapid flow of Spanish he gave directions, and at his words they came over and picked up the trunks. Before long they were out of the door, off to wherever it was Pacho's family lived. Pacho himself turned back to face Mrs. Porter and Nancy.

He bowed deeply. Like a courtier before queens, Nancy thought. Then he stood up, very straight, looking directly at them.

"I thank you," he said, clearly and slowly. "I thank you very much indeed."

He spoke in English. Evidently he thought the gift was

so great that he must use the language of the donors in order to express his gratitude properly.

"Oh, you are quite welcome," Mrs. Porter and Nancy told him.

He left the room, following his friends who were carrying the trunks. When he was gone, Mrs. Porter and Nancy went back to their packing. There was no time to waste; they must be ready for the journey in the morning.

Chapter 7

IT SEEMED to Nancy that she had scarcely closed her eyes before a knock came at the bedroom door.

"Time to get up," Mr. Porter was saying.

Nancy and Mrs. Porter and Betty were off their cots almost before he finished speaking. They dressed hurriedly in the clothes they had laid out the night before. Nancy packed her nightgown into the makeshift saddlebag, and as she did so, heard a slight click. The bottles of medicine were evidently touching each other. She knew she must change them, placing them on the top of the bag, with her gown and Mama's shawl between them. She wondered, as she did so, if Pacho's friend would really be there with the mule, as he had promised. Immediately she pushed the thought aside. As Betty had said, Pacho kept his promises.

And she was right. When they came to the dining room door the next morning, there stood Pacho, a young boy at his side.

"Juan," Pacho said, touching his companion's arm. "Mule . . . you . . ." He pointed to Nancy. Then he motioned to the outside, where a group of mules stood.

"Oh, thank you, Pacho," Nancy said. "And you, Juan."

"My mother, my sister," Pacho went on, "*Muchas gracias.*" He turned to Mrs. Porter, including her in the thanks. "They . . . they like . . ."

"I am glad," Mrs. Porter told him.

"It's time we started," Mr. Porter broke in. "First we eat, and then we leave. The boy, Juan, is it? Tell him."

Nancy, with a bit of help from Pacho, made Juan understand. Then both of the boys went outside and the Porters and Nancy walked into the dining room.

"We are taking our lunches with us," Mr. Porter said, when they were seated at the table. "Saves time. We want to make Cruces by night. Isn't that what you said, Rex?"

Rex nodded. "From there," he went on to explain, "we go by canoes. Bungoes, the natives call them. Down the Chagres River to the town of Chagres. Then we catch the boat to New Orleans."

The waiter came with the lunches, and Nancy reached for her reticule. "How much?" she asked. "Mine and Juan's?"

"Independent little piece, aren't you," Mr. Porter laughed, not seeming at all displeased with her. "One dollar each. He wanted more but we—well, we sort of persuaded him."

He took the money and then said, "You ready?" directing his question to Mrs. Porter.

"Yes," she told him.

"Goody, goody, we're leaving," Mark said, and Betty clapped her hands. They seemed to feel sure that some sort of adventure lay ahead.

"All right, let's get our things out and then we'll be off."

Nancy followed Mrs. Porter back to their room. With one hand she dragged her improvised saddlebag; in her other hand the reticule. Then she hesitated a moment. Both Mr. Porter and Rex had said it was important to keep an eye on your belongings at all times. Why not put the reticule inside the saddlebag? One less thing to look after, that way. Quickly she opened the bag, dropped the reticule on top of the contents, and then closed it tightly once more. Then she dragged it to the door where Juan was waiting. He took it and led the way toward the group of mules, stopping beside one that was standing apart from the others. Then he pointed to her.

"Mine?" she asked. And he said, "*Sí, sí*," and began attaching her saddlebag to the mule's back. She was delighted to see her mount had a sidesaddle. Because of this, the trip would be easier for her. Nancy looked to where the Porters were putting their baggage on their mules and saw that Mrs. Porter, too, had a sidesaddle.

Juan now pointed to a small burro, scarcely bigger than a large shepherd dog. "*Es mío*," he said, and mounted. He had no saddle, only a small blanket on the burro's back. He pointed in the direction they were to take, indicating that he, too, would be one of the party. We might have expected this, Nancy thought. He certainly will want to bring his mule back. She was pleased. The Porters would not need to feel responsible for her. Not today, at any rate. Juan led the mule to a projecting stone, indicating Nancy was to mount there. Mrs. Porter, with Betty riding behind her, was already on her own mule, as was Mr. Porter with Mark behind him. Rex rode by himself. The two natives in command of the Porters' mounts had their own mules. They broke into a torrent of words now, pointing in the direction they were to go.

"Yes," Mr. Porter said. "Let's go."

They were off, down the streets of Panama City, leaving the town. They passed through the narrow streets already filled with people, many no doubt waiting for the next ship to take off to San Francisco and the riches they felt sure were awaiting them. The Porters' guides led the way through the gates of the walls which surrounded the city, and soon the party came to the trail.

Here they rode in single file. First a guide. Then Mrs. Porter and Betty. After them, Nancy. Mr. Porter and Mark next, and behind them, Rex. Finally another guide and then, astride his little burro, Juan. The leader gave a wild whoop. The journey had started.

The trail was narrow, not more than four feet wide. For the most part it was dirt, tightly packed down by the feet of the pack animals that passed over it. Occasionally there were well-worn paving stones.

"Laid by the Spanish years ago," Mr. Porter explained.

"For awhile they pretty well took this place over."

The trail ascended sharply. Before long it seemed they were going almost straight up, directly into the blue sky which arched over them.

"Mama," Betty said, "it's hard to hold to you. I'm almost sliding off backwards."

"So you are, honey," Mrs. Porter said. "Papa," she called out, "I think we should tie Betty to me."

Rex made the guides understand they must stop. He came to his mother, who handed him a shawl she had attached to her saddle. Together they tied it around Betty and then around Mrs. Porter's waist.

"Now you'll stay put," Mrs. Porter told her.

"She looks like a papoose on your back," Mark said. "Remember we saw them when we were with the wagons." It seemed like a good joke to him.

"You know," Mr. Porter said thoughtfully, "we better tie you to me, too." And then quickly, before the boy could argue, "We don't want you falling off and rolling down the mountain."

"There were boy papooses too," Nancy reminded him. "Look . . ." She reached over to her pack, opened it, and from it drew Mama's shawl. "Here's something almost as pretty as Betty has."

Mark looked unconvinced for a moment, and then Rex spoke up firmly. "Go ahead. We can't fool around, Mark."

Mark, without complaint, allowed himself to be tied securely to his father's back, and they were off once more, winding up the narrow path.

Before long, they came to a wider place in the trail, and met another party.

"Where are you going?" one man asked.

"Back home," Mr. Porter told him.

"Find anything?" He pointed toward the direction in which he evidently thought the gold fields lay.

"A little," Mr. Porter told him.

"Bet you're so rich you didn't have to stay any longer. We met a man yesterday who was taking better than fifty thousand dollars home. Dust, and nuggets. Found a real rich lode."

No wonder the Courtneys wanted to get their hands on a map which might lead them to riches such as that, Nancy thought.

"No," Mr. Porter assured the man earnestly. "It's as I told you. I have only a little. Enough to buy a farm and settle down on it."

Nancy could understand why he didn't want anyone to think he was carrying back a fortune.

"Well, you can have your farm," the man said. "It's not for me."

"Guess we better be getting along," Mr. Porter told him. "Want to make Cruces by night."

"Oh, you'll do that all right," the man assured him. "You have downhill the last part of the trail. Goes faster, then."

Each party continued on its own way.

Sometimes the trail was so narrow, groups could not pass when they met. At such times, a guide went ahead to warn any party, if one was coming, to wait. Or, perhaps, to tell them the Porters would do the waiting. At one of these spots, the trees grew so close and thick they formed a green wall on both sides. Parrots flashed back and forth among the limbs, and hordes of other birds, bright of plumage, beautiful to see.

"Look at that one," Mark cried as one with brilliant red feathers flew by, close enough to touch. "I saw it first. It's mine."

Almost immediately it was followed by another bird, this one predominantly blue.

"That's mine," Betty said. And then she added smugly, "Mine is even prettier."

Before Mark could begin any argument about the beauty of his own discovery, Betty began to sing, "Can't get a redbird, a bluebird will do."

Before long, all of them were singing the familiar words of the old song, coming down hard on the lines, "Skip to my Lou, my darling." Their words bounced off the cliffs and came back to them, each echo fainter than the one before had been.

The song helps, Nancy thought. For a short time it took their minds off the discomfort they were enduring. This was certainly not an easy ride, especially for the children, bound so tightly by the shawls that they were scarcely able to move. She herself was finding the experience far from easy. Riding a mule was very different from riding a horse. Horseback riding was almost like being in a rocking chair; on a mule you jolted up and down, like popcorn in a hot skillet. She smiled a little, thinking this, holding tightly to the bridle reins to keep from falling off backward as they climbed the steep path.

"What are you laughing about?" Mark asked.

"I was thinking maybe I should tie myself to the saddle too," she told him, her words coming out a bit unevenly because of the jolting. "To keep me from bouncing off."

Sometimes they had to duck their heads in order to miss the overhanging branches. By and by they were on the wider trail once more. The lead guide came back to confer with Mr. Porter. Much of what he said was gestures, but his meaning came across.

"We're to stop now and eat lunch," Mr. Porter said. "The way I understand it, we're over the Divide."

"The Divide?" Mark asked, from his shawl.

"Yes, the Continental Divide."

"Oh, I know about that," Betty said. "We studied it at school. We'll be going downhill, now."

"Goody. Then I can take off this shawl," Mark said.

"Of course," Mr. Porter assured him. "As soon as we stop for lunch. And don't forget to thank Nancy."

"I already did," Mark said. "When she let me have it."

They dismounted for lunch at the first wide spot in the road. Mark immediately started toward the grassy plot which lined the trail. A guide yanked him back, entirely without ceremony. Before the boy could express the indignation he so plainly felt, Juan joined the group. He pointed to the tree toward which Mark had headed. Hanging from it was a great snake, six or more feet long.

"Probably a boa constrictor," Rex said. Then he looked at the grass beneath the tree. Here were huge tarantulas, rushing about in great haste.

The guides spoke rapidly, directing their words to Nancy. By a dint of listening closely, having them repeat, and asking some questions of her own, she understood the gist of their words.

"They—that snake and those—well, whatever they are—won't hurt us, if we stay away from them."

"Oh, we will," Mrs. Porter assured her. "Don't worry."

They ate their lunch, sitting in the middle of the trail. Actually the place was not too desirable either. Shadowed by the great trees, it was still damp from the rains that had ceased only a few weeks ago. Insects by the hundreds crawled at the trail's edge, many of them acting as if they meant to help themselves to the food at any moment.

Mark took a bite of the meat. "Just like chewing Papa's razor strap," he said. Indeed, the dried strings of beef did have a leathery texture.

"And this," he motioned to the hardtack, "it tastes like a rock."

"Don't complain about your food," Mr. Porter told him.

Privately Nancy agreed with the boy, although she didn't say as much.

"By night we'll be at Cruces," Mr. Porter reminded them. "Maybe we'll have something better there."

Soon they were back on their mounts. The trail was easier for it was going downhill. They wound around rocks, and now and then Nancy could see, far below them, a stream twisting its way through the ravines.

"Is that the Chagres River?" she asked Mr. Porter, and he said he supposed it was.

"Yes," Rex told her. "It is. Tomorrow we'll be on it, in sort of a canoe, headed for the town of Chagres."

It looked inviting, Nancy thought, with the huge trees on both banks. Even from this distance she could see bright spots of color, which she supposed were flowers hanging from the branches. Tomorrow they would be on that stretch of water, riding between the flower festooned trees. A lot better than bouncing along on a mule's back.

They came to Cruces late in the afternoon. For the most part the town seemed to be made up of bamboo or thatched huts. But Nancy saw what looked like a church in the background. Not far from it was a large frame building, somewhat dilapidated.

"I imagine that's where we'll stay tonight," Mr. Porter said, pointing toward the building.

Rex said he felt sure it was; the guides were making their way toward it.

Several men were standing at the door of the building when the Porters and Nancy came to it. "Good evening," one of them said. "I'm Phillip Barnes, from Iowa."

"And I am Ned Porter, and this is my wife and children." Then he added quickly, "And a friend, Miss Nancy Sullivan."

Mr. Barnes introduced the three men with him. "You came from Panama," he continued, making it a statement, not a question. Where else would anyone be coming from on this trail?

"Yes," Mr. Porter told him. "Left early this morning."

The mule drivers stood by, saying nothing. Perhaps they even anticipated the next question.

"These mules," Mr. Barnes asked, "and the drivers. How have they been?"

"Quite satisfactory," Mr. Porter assured him.

"Do you suppose we could hire them to take us back to Panama City?"

Even as he spoke half a dozen other men, evidently having the same idea in mind, were pushing toward the group. As Rex had said, there was no end to the people who were anxious to go to Panama City. No wonder there had been little difficulty in hiring drivers to come this far. They stood quietly now, realizing they were in demand and they had no reason to push their services off on anyone.

"I assume you are headed for Chagres," Mr. Barnes said.

"Yes," Mr. Porter told him.

"Have you already made arrangements for your transportation?"

Rex broke in, "We did that before we left Panama City."

"Excuse me for saying so, but you can't believe a word these guides say. Tell you they'll show up, so I hear, and then, like as not, go off in another direction. Do you see any boatmen waiting here for you?"

"Well," Rex said. "No . . ." He looked embarrassed at having to make the admission.

"Don't feel bad," Mr. Barnes told him. "It's not your fault. It's happened to a lot of people."

Rex relaxed a little at this, and Nancy felt grateful to Mr. Barnes.

"We were lucky to have a good crew," Mr. Barnes said. He pointed in the direction of a group sitting nearby on the ground. "The Captain on the ship which brought us to Chagres recommended them. We found we could trust them. Their leader is named Miguel, and he managed everything very well indeed."

"Good," Mr. Porter said.

"And you say these men that brought you over were reliable," Mr. Barnes went on.

"Yes." Plainly Mr. Porter wasn't committing his group to anything until he knew the details.

"What I'm trying to say is this," Mr. Barnes continued. "If you think your group is dependable, we'll ask them to take us on. And, if you want our crew to take you to Chagres, we'll recommend you to them."

Mr. Porter and Rex looked at each other. Evidently they read agreement in each other's faces.

"All right," Mr. Porter said, "if Rex thinks it's a good idea, it will suit me."

"I am sure they'll be glad to have the job," Mr. Barnes assured them. "Not many people going to Chagres. Now with us, it's different."

"That's what we've been told," Mr. Porter laughed.

"I suppose you are spending the night here," Mr. Barnes said. "It's really the only place."

Mr. Porter said yes, that was what they had been told. And he guessed they might as well go in.

Juan came forward now. He held the bridle reins while Nancy slipped out of the saddle. For a moment she thought she was too weary even to stand up, much less walk the few steps into the rooming house.

"It might be well for us to have some papers drawn up," Mr. Barnes was saying. "You with our group to row you on to Chagres and us with your guides to take us to Panama City. This is supposed to be the surest way to work things out. The—what do you call him? The Mayor writes them out and we and they sign."

"The *alcalde*," Nancy said.

Mr. Barnes turned to her quickly. "Yes, that's it. You speak Spanish?"

"Only a little," she told him honestly. She could see the crew looking at her with new respect. It was not an entirely unpleasant sensation for her.

"*Hablo español también,*" Mark broke in importantly. The native oarsmen seemed truly impressed now. They looked at Mark, and then at each other.

"That's fine," Mr. Barnes said. Evidently he was impressed too. "Now let's all go over to the rooming house— my crew, your trail drivers, and us. Then we can send for the . . ."

"*Alcalde,*" Betty broke in, not wanting to be left out.

"Yes, the *alcalde.*" Mr. Barnes stumbled only a little over the word. "He can draw up contracts. In the morning we can leave."

Nancy was elected to convey the information to both groups of natives. They seemed to understand, for several followed the Porters and Mr. Barnes across to the rooming house.

The proprietor spoke English. Not fluently, but enough so they could understand him. Yes, he could put them up for the night. Three dollars apiece for supper, lodging, and breakfast.

"And will he ask the Mayor to come and write the contract?" Mr. Barnes asked, turning to Nancy.

"The *alcalde* . . ." Nancy explained to the owner of the rooming house. She tried to tell him they wanted the *alcalde* to draw up a contract between them and the oarsmen, and the trail drivers. She designated each group with a wave of her hand.

The proprietor said, "Yes, yes, he does such things," and sent a boy who had been lounging near the door away on what was evidently an errand calculated to bring back the Mayor.

Nancy began to feel more uncomfortable by the minute. Would she be capable of handling this situation? She managed all right with Pacho, but then, he understood a little English. They could always fill in with gestures. Besides, nothing of great importance was at stake there.

"Now, your rooms," the proprietor said. "*Alcalde,* soon."

They were assigned their rooms, Nancy, Mrs. Porter, and Betty together; Mr. Porter, Rex, and Mark in another one—an arrangement quite acceptable to all. By the time they deposited their luggage, a boy came to the door to say the *alcalde* had arrived.

Rex turned to Nancy. "You'll come with us?" he asked.

"Me, too," Mark said.

"All right," Mr. Porter agreed. And then, seeing Betty's stricken face, "Come on."

They trooped down to meet the Mayor, in the room which passed for the office of the boarding house. With each step they took, Nancy felt added uncertainty.

Scarcely had they come into the room when a man entered the front door. He looked at the proprietor, who motioned toward Nancy.

"Greetings, *Señorita,*" the man said to Nancy. "*Habla español?*"

"*Un poco,*" she told him. "A little . . ."

"It is—to write a—a contract?" he asked.

He did know English too, Nancy thought with relief.

Perhaps together they could work things out. Maybe she wasn't needed at all. Still, she would not soon forget the look of respect on the faces of the crew, including Miguel, the man who was the designated leader. The fact that she and Mark and Betty could speak a little Spanish made them all regard the party with a little more respect.

"Sí . . . they," she gestured toward the leader, "take us—" she pointed toward the Porters and herself—"to Chagres. *Escriba* . . . write . . ." She knew she wasn't getting it exactly as it should be said, but the *alcalde* seemed to understand.

"Us, too," Mr. Barnes prompted her.

"And them—" she pointed to Mr. Barnes and his party— "to Panama City."

"Sí. Have done before." The *alcalde* seemed very proud of himself, whether because he could draw up a contract or was able to express himself in English, Nancy couldn't be sure.

He took from his pocket a pen and some pieces of paper. With a flourish he went over to the hotel desk and there wrote on two papers. These he brought back to Nancy. On one she could see the word, "Panama City," on the other, "Chagres." She recognized also the word for boat, "bungo," and on the other, what she took to be "mules."

"I think it is all right," she told Mr. Porter. "Remember, I know only a little Spanish. I could be wrong in saying these contracts are exactly as they should be."

"We trust you," Mr. Barnes said.

Mr. Porter and Rex nodded.

"*Nombre,*" the *alcalde* said, pointing to the paper. "You are to sign your names."

Nancy turned to Mr. Barnes and Mr. Porter.

"*Sí*—names . . ."

The men stepped over, put their signatures on the proper contracts. Then the *alcalde* signaled for the leader of the mule team and for Miguel, the one at the head of the boatmen, to come forward. This they did, and affixed a sign which Nancy supposed stood for the name of each. One contract was handed to Mr. Barnes, the other to Mr. Porter.

The *alcalde* stood there, waiting.

"How much?" Mr. Barnes asked.

The *alcalde* held up one finger. "Dollar . . ."

"He says one dollar, in our money." Nancy turned to Mr. Porter.

"Oh, yes . . ."

Mr. Porter and Mr. Barnes each handed the *alcalde* a dollar. The man said, "*Gracias,* thanks." Then he turned to the men before him—the trail drivers and the boatmen —and began a rapid set of instructions in Spanish. Nancy understood enough to know he was telling them they must come through with their part of the bargain, or they would hear from him. They nodded understandingly.

"Tomorrow, you go," the *alcalde* told them. "Be early— where bungo and mules leave . . ."

There was another rapid interchange of instructions.

Yes, they knew when to leave. Yes, they would be there on time.

Finally the business seemed to be finished. Mr. Barnes turned to Nancy.

"Because you knew Spanish, I think we have a better contract. One with people we can trust. Thank you."

"I really did very little," Nancy said, but she was still pleased he would say this to her.

"It was enough to make them know we were capable of understanding them, be it only a little," Mr. Barnes told her. "Now, good night. And, if I don't see you again, good-by and good luck."

He walked out of the room toward his own quarters, followed by the men who made up his party.

"Time we went to our rooms, too," Mr. Porter said. "We'll be off early in the morning."

Chapter 8

"MAMA," Mark said, pointing to the men rowing the bungo, "they don't have any clothes on."

"Sh . . ." Mrs. Porter hushed him automatically, although the child came close to speaking the truth.

Actually, they wore very little. Breechclouts, really. They stood, one at each end of the bungo, dipping their long oars into the water. Even though it was still early morning, their bare chests glistened with perspiration.

The bungo, making its way down the Chagres River, was really nothing more than a crude canoe which appeared to have been carved out of a single great tree trunk. The baggage was piled in a pyramid in the center. On one side of it sat Nancy, Mrs. Porter, and Betty. On the other, Mr. Porter, Rex, and Mark, all crowded close together. At each end were the oarsmen, two rowing, two sitting there evidently waiting to take their turn. Over the top of the bungo was a canopy of palm leaves.

"*Toldo*," Miguel said, addressing himself to Nancy. Then he pointed to the sky, and she knew he was trying to tell her the *toldo* was there in order to protect them from the sun.

"*Sí*," she said. It was all to the good that he knew she spoke Spanish, be it ever so little. Of course he and his crew had recommendations from the *alcalde*, but even so . . .

Giant palm trees grew on both sides of the river, and among and around and between them were other trees whose name there was no way of guessing. From them came a constant chattering of monkeys and the screaming of parrots. Sometimes a great log had fallen into the river, making it necessary to work the boat around it carefully.

"Look, Mama," Mark cried out, "that log opened its mouth. Wide . . ."

Actually it wasn't a log at all, although it did look like one. Rather, it was a huge alligator lying in the shallow water at the edge of the river. Betty shivered a little and pushed closer to her mother.

"It won't hurt you, honey," Mrs. Porter comforted her. "See . . . it's there by the riverbank and we are here in the boat—safe."

Nancy could understand the child's fright. She herself could almost see the bungo, together with all its passengers, disappearing into the huge, gaping mouth. At that moment, a blood-curdling howl sounded from the dense greenness of the shore.

"Jaguar," Rex explained.

Even recognizing the source of the sound didn't make it any more pleasant.

Nancy did not know exactly when she began to realize that one of the oarsmen was not taking his turn at rowing. Instead, he lay still, saying nothing, making no move. Was he lazy? What was his excuse for being in the bungo if he were not helping? Miguel evidently knew the boy, for he had spoken to him when he boarded, calling him Abel.

She caught Rex's eyes on the reclining boy. Plainly he too felt the matter should be investigated.

"Ask them," Rex signaled to Nancy.

She turned to the oarsman standing directly behind the boy. "*Qué?*" she asked. "What?"

He hesitated, trying to find a way to express the nature of the difficulty. Then, evidently thinking he could act out the explanation better than he could say it, he put his hand to his own stomach and pointed to the boy lying in the boat.

"Abel . . ." Again he went through a series of gestures, indicating the boy was sick.

Sick! Nancy tried not to show the concern she felt. All the stories of fever victims came rushing in on her. The people who had become ill on the trail across the Isthmus, and other places as well.

Zeke. Mama.

She knew the Porters were thinking the same thing. No

need to translate to them. They too had understood both
the gesture and the words. They also had personal knowledge of the dreaded fever. Had not Mr. Porter been ill
with it in Panama City, making it necessary for Rex to
take over the arrangements? Nancy moved uneasily, trying to brush away the thoughts that came to her. When
she did so, her shoulder touched her bag. As if they were
there for the sake of comforting her, the solid outlines of
Mama's medicine bottles pushed against her. Like a flash,
the idea came to her.

Turning quickly, she opened her bag. From it she took
one of the bottles of medicine. She removed the cork and
then looked around for something into which she could
pour the dose. Mr. Porter, understanding what she was
about to do, drew a spoon from his own bag.

"Here," he said, handing it to her.

She poured the medicine into the spoon. Then she
turned to the boy. Whether he was sick or only pretending,
the dosage would do him no harm.

"Abel," she said, remembering that was the name they
had called him. "*Bueno.*" She made a gesture in the gen-
eral direction of his stomach. "*Muy bueno.*"

She could feel everyone's eyes on her. The Porters. The
other oarsmen. Abel, seeming reluctant to take the medicine. Miguel said a few quick, staccato words. Abel hesitated only a moment longer and then, with a sullen look
on his face, opened his mouth and swallowed the contents
of the spoon.

Nancy started to replace the bottle in her bag, but before she could do so, Rex said quietly, "Leave it out. He may need another dose."

Nancy understood him fast enough. If Abel was only pretending to be sick, the medicine would give him less excuse to lie there doing nothing. If he were really ill, it might help him.

Everyone on the bungo was very quiet, even the oarsmen. They knew quite well the possibilities of the situation which faced them. Nancy hesitated only a moment. Then, slowly and deliberately so that everyone—even Abel —could see what she was doing, she put the bottle and the spoon on the top of her bag where she could reach them quickly and without difficulty.

The river had grown very narrow here; so narrow, in fact, that they could have reached out and touched the lush greenness on each side had they wished to do so. Mr. Porter, probably wanting to take their minds off the threat posed by Abel's illness, said, "Men working on the railroad say this stuff grows so fast everything they cut down one day is back by morning."

"Look, Mama," Betty cried. She pointed to some butterflies, huge and bright as floating flowers.

For the time being, they all seemed to forget about Abel, still lying at the end of the bungo, giving no indication as to whether the medicine had any effect on him.

The river had grown wider, which was fortunate, for another bungo was coming toward them.

"Headed for Chagres?" one of the passengers called out.

"Yes," Mr. Porter said.

"You're going in the wrong direction. Better come with us to California."

"We've been there," Mr. Porter told him, not explaining any more. No need trying to call across the distance that was growing wider between them.

Anyway, at that moment Miguel indicated it was time to stop. He spoke to the other oarsmen in a jargon Nancy did not even try to understand. In almost no time at all the bungo was anchored, and all of them except Abel clambered out. How good it was, Nancy thought, to be free of those cramped quarters, even though briefly. Led by Miguel, who apparently planned this stop ahead of time, they made their way to a small shelter, really nothing more than a thatched roof over some poles. Once here, Miguel spread out their lunch on a crude table fashioned from a log.

They all turned their attention to the food. Jerked beef again and hardtack. They drank the water Miguel had brought with them. Mark, doubtless warned by his mother's swift glance, merely showed his distaste but said nothing. They walked around a bit, just for the sake of stretching their legs and then made their way back to the bungo. Abel lay still, not even seeming to notice their return.

"Another dose?" Rex asked.

Nancy said yes, and again reached for her bottle and

the spoon. This time the boy made no objections to taking the medicine. Nancy caught Miguel's eyes on her, and thought she saw approval in them.

Once more the bungo started down the river. Occasionally the oarsmen began to sing, more a chant than music. The riverbanks dashed the echoes back, giving an eerie quality to the sound. Mark and Betty grew drowsy and slept, Mark leaning against his father, Betty against her mother. An afternoon hush settled over the river. It was as if all life on and around it—birds and insects and animals—was also resting. Even the oarsmen became quiet.

Rex pointed to the medicine bottle again, and Nancy reached for it. Abel seemed quite willing this time, moving toward the spoon as if he welcomed the dose. He does look better, Nancy thought. Perhaps he was really sick, not pretending.

Nancy found that she too was growing drowsy. She must have gone to sleep, for the next thing she was conscious of was a touch on her shoulder. She jerked herself awake, for a moment not realizing where she was. The sight of Miguel bending over her awakened her fast enough. The shadows were deepening now. It was late afternoon.

"*Noche,*" he told her. "*Aquí.*" He pointed toward the shore.

"*Sí,*" she said, and then turned to explain to the Porters. "He says we are to spend the night here."

"I judged as much," Mr. Porter said. "Now, stay close together."

They left the boat, stepped out on the dock which extended over the river. Mr. Porter and Rex, assisted by two of the oarsmen, carried the baggage. Miguel, who probably thought such work was not for him, and Abel did not offer to help. When they were all off the boat, Miguel tied it securely to the wharf and then leaned over to say a few words to Abel who nodded briefly and finally, after a few moments' hesitation, stood up and took his place behind the rest of the party. Then Miguel came to lead them to whatever their destination might be.

The path they followed wound up a hill, through dense vegetation. Now and then they passed a native hut with people standing in front of it and children playing outside. Monkeys, some of them fastened to the huts, chattered incessantly. Birds flew back and forth with a busy fluttering of wings. An oriole nest, almost three feet in length and beautifully woven, hung from a tree branch. In another tree a dove cooed softly.

"Sounds like home," Mrs. Porter said.

"Whee, look!" Mark cried.

He had good reason to call their attention to the strange creature by the side of the path. It looked like a lizard, but surely no lizard ever grew to be this size.

"It must be all of six feet long," Mr. Porter marveled.

"And most of it is tail," Mark said. He was right. The tail was at least two-thirds of the creature's length.

Miguel smiled broadly at the child's reaction. "Iguana," he said.

"Iguana, iguana," Mark repeated after him. "You gotta lotta tail."

Everyone laughed at that, even the oarsmen who realized he had said something supposed to be funny.

They were still laughing when Miguel stopped before a latticed hut and indicated they were to enter. With a bit of sign language and some interpretation by Nancy, they learned this was to be their lodging for the night. They could go inside now, leave their baggage, and then eat.

The interior was no more attractive than was the outside. The hut had reeds for a floor covering. In the middle was a partition of sorts, reaching up perhaps as high as a man's head. In both divisions were three hammocks, each attached to poles driven into the ground.

Mrs. Porter looked at the guides uncertainly. Mr. Porter spoke up hastily, of course realizing it was best to stop any comment she would make. At least they had a place to stay. Under a roof, not out with the crawling reptiles of the forest.

Nancy, Mrs. Porter, and Betty were on one side of the partition, their baggage with them. Mark was greatly pleased to see that he had again been placed with the men.

"I can't wait for supper," he said loftily.

Nancy did not share his anticipation, feeling that the surroundings gave little promise of an appetizing meal. She washed her hands and face with the water provided in the hut. She smoothed her hair, and wished she could have a bath and a complete change of clothes. This was not practical though, because there was really no provision for this in the hut. She would follow the Porters' example and wear the same dress she had traveled in since leaving Panama City. She did, however, unfasten her bag and take out the reticule. She carried it with her as she followed the others to the dining room, a tent with a plank floor and a rough table made of a log smoothed out on top. Logs had also been converted into chairs. Miguel indicated they were to be seated, and when they had taken their places, native boys brought in trays of food.

To Nancy's surprise and, she suspected, to the surprise of the Porters as well, the food was good. There was a bowl of something, she couldn't tell whether it was fruit or vegetable, which Miguel made them understand came from the palm tree. Another platter held meat. Nancy took a bite and found it was delicious, as tender and tasty as chicken. At her inquiring glance, Miguel said, "Iguana . . ."

"But not its tail," Betty said. "That wouldn't fit on the plate. It's good," she went on. "Delicious."

Perhaps it's because we really expected the same old jerked beef again, Nancy thought. No, Betty was right. The food was really excellent, as well as being a welcome change from what they had been eating.

The meal finished, they came outside into complete darkness. Mrs. Porter remarked about it.

"It was daylight when we went in," she said.

"In the tropics," Rex told her, "night comes down like a shooting star."

"That's all right," Mrs. Porter said. "I'm tired enough to go to bed anyway."

Everyone agreed with her, so they went inside to their hammock beds.

"Remember, we start very early in the morning," Mr. Porter reminded them, calling over the partition which divided the sleeping quarters.

Mrs. Porter said yes, she knew that, and then she turned to Nancy. "I think I'll take off only my dress and my shoes," she said. "That way I can dress quicker in the morning."

She probably feels the way I do, Nancy thought. These hammocks aren't really beds, and not worth undressing for. She wondered if any of them would sleep at all, hanging here in mid-air. She wondered too if Abel would be with them again tomorrow and, if he were, would he be feeling better. Perhaps Miguel would leave him here, since he was not helping with the rowing.

That was the last conscious thought she had. The next thing she knew, Mr. Porter was calling to them, "Time to get up," and everyone was out of his hammock and outside the door of the hut in almost no time at all.

Breakfast, although not as good as the food had been the evening before, was still edible. Then once more they were down at the bungo ready to go.

Abel was already there, sitting at the end of the boat.

He looked better, although he did not take his turn row-ing. Miguel pointed to him and then to Nancy, tilting his head back and going through the motion of swallowing. She understood fast enough and spooned out another dose of medicine. Again, the boy took it without protest; he even seemed anxious to have it.

They were off now, in what was practically a repetition of yesterday's journey. Grass and underbrush and trees growing in green profusion on both banks of the river. Flowers blooming brightly. Birds and monkeys and wild life in the trees and on the ground. At noon they again stopped, anchoring the bungo and getting out for lunch. The shelter toward which Miguel led them was much like the one used the day before. Apparently this was a part of the guide service they had contracted for. Nancy felt sure everyone was grateful, as she was, even for the brief chance to be out of the cramped quarters of the bungo.

As was the case yesterday, the food and water was brought from the same kitchen which had prepared their last night's dinner.

"Gee, I hope it's iguana," Mark said. It wasn't, but even so was appetizing.

After lunch, with no explanation to anyone, Abel stepped forward and reached for the oar Miguel had been using. They talked together, briefly, in a language that did not seem to be Spanish. At least, it was entirely unfamiliar to Nancy. The boy nodded his head several times, and finally Miguel left him and went to sit at the end of the bungo, the place Abel had been occupying.

They were late stopping that evening. Perhaps it was because Abel was slower than Miguel and the others or, what was more likely, they were waiting until they came to the place scheduled ahead of time for the night's lodging.

Here they were taken to a tent, little more than an excuse for shelter. By comparison, last night's hut seemed luxurious. This time, food was brought to their tent—fat meat, bread which looked and tasted mouldy, and beans. They barely touched it. When they had finished eating, Nancy, Mrs. Porter, and Betty stretched out, fully dressed, on the pallets spread on the dirt floor. Nobody complained, however. Nancy thought they were more than likely feeling as she did, that this place, unattractive though it might be, was still one day nearer their destination.

Then, late in the afternoon of the fifth day of their trip, they came to their journey's end.

"Chagres," Miguel said, pointing toward the town.

It lay before them. Native huts, bamboo-thatched, set in the green hills as if they had grown there with the other vegetation. Sea gulls circled low.

"They mew like kittens," Betty said.

The gray-green sea edged into the river, turned yellow, then dark brown as it took on the color of the water it flowed into. Miguel pointed toward a two-story building with an overhanging balcony.

"Hotel," he said. "American . . ."

Nancy asked him if they were to stay there.

"*Sí*. Boat . . . New Orleans."

"Hurrah," Mark yelled. "We really are on the way home."

As soon as the bungo stopped, they all were busy locating their own baggage, seeming to feel the way Mark did —that they couldn't wait to be out of these small, cramped quarters, into the hotel and then, as soon as it was possible, bound for New Orleans.

Miguel tied the bungo to the wharf. Abel smiled and looked at Nancy. Perhaps he is trying to say a big "thank you" for making him well again, she thought. The Porters were assembling their baggage, but when Nancy reached for hers, Abel shook his head and took it himself.

Nancy felt a moment of hesitation. The reticule was still in her bag. Should she stop Abel now, open the bag, and remove the reticule? She considered the matter and finally decided that in doing this she might call attention to the fact that it contained something very valuable. If she tried carrying the bag herself, either Mr. Porter or Rex would probably feel that one of them should offer to help her. She decided it would be better to let Abel carry it as they made their way to the hotel, and to keep a close eye on it herself.

Nancy noticed a boy about Abel's age standing on the

wharf. He called out a greeting, and Abel turned to him quickly, giving what was apparently some definite directions. The boy nodded a couple of times, and then was off like a streak.

There was a great deal of confusion on the wharf. People were crowded together so closely it was almost impossible to move among them. Nancy was concentrating on staying with Abel. Certainly she did not want to lose sight of him in the crowd. Amid this babble of voices it would be impossible to call out to him, or even to the Porters. She must keep her eyes on the boy until, finally, they came to the hotel.

She followed him off the wharf, up a path so narrow they must walk in single file. It seemed to be taking a long time to get to the hotel; at first sight she had thought it was nearer the wharf. She was grateful for the quietness here. The noise at the wharf was enough to burst one's eardrums.

The path took a sharp turn now, and Nancy became aware of something that sent a chill through her blood, down to the very depths of her being.

Neither the hotel nor the Porters were anywhere in sight. Instead, she and Abel seemed to be headed into the jungle, away from town.

I mustn't panic, Nancy told herself. Maybe it's just another route to the hotel.

Even as she tried to convince herself of this, she knew she was wrong. She and Abel were going away from the

others. The sound of voices, the confusion, grew fainter
and fainter. Now there were only the monkeys chattering,
the parakeets screaming, and the swish of the underbrush
as the boy pushed it aside.

I should turn around and run back, Nancy thought
wildly.

But what direction would she go if she did run? She had
taken little notice of the route they traveled, being more
concerned with keeping her eyes on Abel and her bag. If
she did set off by herself, she could wind up in a jungle
even more dense. There might be boa constrictors to close
in on her. The guides had said these reptiles never hurt
anyone who did not bother them, but how were they to
know she had no evil intentions against them? And she
must admit that, as yet, Abel had shown no wish to harm
her in any way.

"Abel," she cried out, her voice a part of the chorus of
the jungle, "Abel! *Dónde,* where?"

He did not act as if he heard her. Then she realized
that he had never spoken a word of Spanish. The com-
munication between him and Miguel had been in sylla-
bles, ones that did not sound like any language Nancy had
ever heard. There was no way for her to talk with him
and find out where they were going. She might as well
face that fact, and quit trying to question him.

Still he walked ahead, never hesitating. At least he
knew exactly where they were going. He made an abrupt
turn. Only a few paces from the path they came to a small

bamboo hut. A donkey was tied to a palm tree, the inevitable monkeys clambered about in its branches.

Abel stopped abruptly at the door. Then he turned to Nancy and motioned for her to enter.

I won't budge, she told herself wildly. I won't take one single step into the place. How do I know what is inside?

He stood quietly, waiting for her to enter. There was no impatience in his face. Rather, a sort of entreaty, as if, across the barrier of language, he was begging her to do as he said. Something in his action served to allay her fears. Hesitating only a moment longer, Nancy stooped and entered the low doorway of the hut. Abel followed her, still carrying her bag.

As she stood straight, she noticed there was almost nothing inside. A crude table. A couple of makeshift chairs. And, in one corner, a pallet on which a woman lay. Beside her was a girl, her resemblance to Abel so striking that Nancy felt sure they must be brother and sister.

Abel began speaking directly to the woman on the pallet who listened intently. The younger one nodded each time he spoke, first to him and then at Nancy. The woman on the pallet turned now to regard Nancy searchingly. Nancy had the strange feeling that neither the woman nor the girl was surprised at seeing her. Perhaps they were accustomed to Abel's bringing strangers to the hut. Or maybe they took for granted anything he decided to do and went along with him as a matter of course.

Abel turned and spoke to the girl. She nodded quickly,

and then went out of the hut. He then directed his attention to Nancy, motioning toward one of the crude chairs. She dropped down, welcoming the opportunity. Suddenly she realized she probably could not have remained standing another moment. She did not know whether this exhaustion came from fright or weariness. Certainly she had good reason for both.

Presently the girl was back with a tray in her hands. It was lined with green leaves, perhaps those of the banana plant, and over it a covering of the same kind. She carried it carefully, with an air that was almost ceremonial. The woman on the pallet watched, approval and pride in her glance. Whatever was being done gave them all a sense of great satisfaction. Plainly this was no ordinary rite in which they were engaged.

Nancy could see steam coming up from among the green leaves which covered the tray. Apparently, she was about to be offered food. Seeing it, she realized how very hungry she was. For the last few days she had eaten little, comforting herself with the promise that, once they were in Chagres, they would have something they could eat with relish.

The girl set the dish on the table before Nancy now. Abel moved over, bowed deeply, and then removed the green leaves from the top of the tray. Nancy drew back in horror. It wasn't . . . it couldn't be!

A tiny form, browned and roasted to a fine degree of

doneness, lay on the platter. It looked like nothing so much as a doll-sized baby.

At that moment she heard the sound of drums in the distance. They drew nearer. From somewhere back in her mind there came the memory of the stories Papa had read to her about the cannibals who played their drums while going through the rites of human sacrifice. Was she supposed to take part in such a ritual now? She drew back, making a gesture as if to rise from the table. What did it matter if she ran out of here, into the jungle? Better to be lost there than to take part in what was going on here.

Something about her terror, her great fear, seemed to carry through to Abel. Almost too quickly for eye to follow, he was out of the hut and then back again. This time he carried with him a monkey, evidently the family pet, which had been just outside the door. He pointed to it, and then to the food on her plate. Monkey! Her relief at knowing she had been wrong in her first assumption helped overcome her horror. Her dislike for the dish before her was not as great as the fear she had of what might happen if she rejected it. She felt she must taste it.

She took a reluctant bite, feeling sure she could not swallow it, that it would remain forever there in her throat, blocking all other food she might ever try to eat again.

Actually, it did not taste at all bad. She could manage to swallow a bite. Abel was watching her with pleasure. She took another bite.

The drums were nearer; they seemed to have stopped

just outside the hut. Abel and the girl looked at Nancy, and then at her plate. She stood up, indicating her meal was finished. Abel went to the door and gave some sort of signal. Then he stepped aside to admit two men, both dressed in a regalia Nancy could not identify. Certainly she had never seen anything like it before. Over their shoulders were strung festoons of bright feathers and beads. Their faces were painted until they resembled great masks.

They looked at her briefly and then turned and walked toward the pallet. Once there, they began to chant, their voices in turn sounding like a dirge and then a cry of triumph. They picked up the pallet, the woman still lying on it. She did not seem in the least disturbed or even surprised as they carried her outside.

The drums sounded even louder. Abel pointed to Nancy, his meaning clear. She was supposed to follow them. For a moment she hung back, although really she had no choice, for he and the girl were directly behind her, almost pushing her out of the hut.

She blinked a little, once they were outside. A number of natives were crowded around the edge of the hut. Some half-dozen drummers, all wearing headdresses of feathers, were pounding away with a deafening rhythm. Others—men, women and children—stood close by. They made way for Nancy to pass through, Abel close behind her. Only a moment, and the two of them came to where the woman lay on her pallet, the men who had carried her out standing beside her. Once Nancy and Abel were there, the ring of people closed again.

This can't be me, Nancy was thinking. Nancy Sullivan who grew up in Illinois with Papa and Mama to watch over me. Safe. Protected.

Abel touched her arm and she jumped back, looking up at him with terror in her eyes. Then she saw he was holding her bag. He pointed to it, indicating that she should open it. Does he know the reticule, with its nuggets and gold dust is in there, she thought wildly. Then an even more frightening idea came to her. Had the Courtneys sent him? Was this a plot, with Miguel a part of it?

Again he touched her arm, and on his face there was nothing sinister. Something about his attitude reassured her. Besides, she felt she had no choice, really. She leaned over, untied the string that held the bag shut. For a moment she considered pushing the reticule down farther among the other contents, but discarded the idea, thinking it might only serve to call attention to the fact that it contained something she considered extremely valuable. Instead, she looked at the boy for further instruction.

From his pocket he drew a spoon, the same one she had used to give him his doses there on the bungo. Someway, sometime, he had managed to get possession of it. He held it out to her, then pointed toward his mother while he went through the motions of swallowing.

Nancy understood and, understanding, was less frightened. She took out the medicine, being careful to close the bag once the bottle was removed, and when Abel handed her the spoon, she tilted the bottle and poured some of the liquid into it.

The noise of the drums and the chanting grew louder now. The woman lifted her head, and when Nancy held the spoon to her lips, swallowed the medicine quickly. Abel again lifted his hand to his mouth, and pointed to the woman, indicating another dose should be given. Nancy filled the spoon, extended it toward the woman, who swallowed the contents without question. As she did so, the people watching began a chant of their own. Nancy replaced the cork in the bottle.

And then, above the chanting, the beat of drums, she heard another sound. Out of the darkness, just beyond the hut, a voice was calling.

"Nancy . . . Nancy . . ."

She broke through the circle of natives, dragging her bag after her. She was conscious of several people there in the narrow path which led to the hut, but she had eyes for only one of them.

"Rex," she cried, dropping the bag, throwing her arms around him, holding tight as a drowning person might hold to someone who had come to the rescue. "Rex . . ."

"There, there, Nancy," he said. "We're here. Everything's all right."

Still she clung to him. Then, after a few moments, he reached up and gently took her hands away from his shoulders.

"It's time we started back to the hotel," he told her. "Basil will lead us."

He turned to a man standing beside him. "This is Basil Conner," he said. "He's an American, with the mail service line. Now, let's go."

He picked up her bag, and the three of them walked down the path in the direction Nancy felt sure the hotel was located.

Chapter 9

$\mathcal{T}$HEY SAT in the Porters' room at the hotel, filling in the details of what had happened, not keeping the story in any logical order, breaking in on each other. Mr. and Mrs. Porter were there, and Rex and Nancy and Basil Conner.

"We put the children to bed," Mrs. Porter said. "I didn't want them to see how worried I was." She reached out and squeezed Nancy's hand.

"I hate to tell you, Nancy," Mr. Porter said. "We didn't really miss you until we got here, to the hotel. Then Mark looked around and asked, 'Where's Nancy?' We just stood and stared at each other."

"It was awful." Mrs. Porter's voice trembled a little. "Almost like having Betty or Mark missing."

"It wasn't your fault," Nancy assured her. "I should have been watching. I wasn't thinking of anything except keeping up with Abel, and then . . ."

"We didn't know what to do," Mr. Porter told her.

"Without you, we couldn't talk to Miguel and ask him what happened. The last we had seen of you, Abel was holding your bag, waiting for the rest of us to leave the bungo."

"You should have heard the commotion," Mrs. Porter went on. "We had the hotel lobby in an uproar. Miguel was standing there, looking helpless and frightened. We tried to talk to him, but of course you know he speaks no English. And the children's Spanish—well, they didn't know enough to help out much. Besides, they were too upset to talk. Then Mr. Conner offered to help."

"I realized there was some difficulty, so I came over to see if I could be of any assistance," Basil Conner said. "When they told me what had happened, I thought Miguel might give us some explanation. I know him. He's trustworthy. I often recommend him to people who want a guide to Cruces."

He continued his explanation. Miguel knew Abel and his family. That was why he allowed the boy to stay on the bungo even when he was not helping.

"He did not have the Isthmus fever," Basil Conner explained. "Miguel would not have allowed him to expose you people, had that been the case. As nearly as I could gather, his sickness was the result of having the wrong food, or perhaps no food at all. Abel had been without work for some time and had come to Cruces hoping to find something."

Miguel knew the family needed money. The father was

dead, the mother was sick. Nancy's medicine had helped Abel. Perhaps the boy had taken Nancy to his mother, thinking the medicine might also work its magic there.

"Why didn't he tell Nancy?" Mr. Porter asked. "He knew she spoke Spanish. Seems to me he could have made her understand instead of kidnapping her."

"He doesn't speak Spanish," Basil Conner explained. "He's a mixture of Indian and some Jamaican and goodness knows what else. These people have a jargon all their own. But Miguel speaks their language, and Spanish also. Since I speak Spanish, I was able to talk with him. He told me we should not worry. The boy would not harm Miss Nancy; by and by he would bring her back."

"Only," Rex said quietly, "we weren't going to wait for that. We told Miguel to take us to Abel's home. Then we could see for ourselves if you were there. So, we came."

Nancy shuddered a little, remembering. How was she to know Abel meant no harm; how could she even guess anyone would be able to find her? How was she to know the sick woman was his mother?

"Was it pretty bad, honey?" Mrs. Porter asked.

"Well . . ." She tried to tell them what had happened to her. The terror she felt when she first realized she was separated from the Porters and headed—where, she did not know—along with Abel. Her fear when they came at last to the hut. The meal they served her.

"It looked like a—well, like a baby lying there on the

plate," Nancy said. She explained how Abel made her know what it really was.

"Monkey," Mrs. Porter gasped, horrified at the very thought.

"I managed to eat a couple of bites," Nancy said. "I could see it meant a lot to all of them. And, well, I was afraid not to, really."

"That was a great honor," Basil Conner told her. "It is a dish reserved for special guests."

"Then the drums began to sound, and two men came into the hut," Nancy went on. She described the ritual. The chanting, the dancing, the drums. "A nightmare," she said. "Only I was awake. And there was nobody I could talk to about it."

"Abel thought you'd understand," Basil Conner told her.

"Understand?"

Rex looked at him. "You tell her," he said. "She should know."

"Well, you see it's like this." Basil hesitated a moment, plainly searching for the right words. "He thought you were a witch doctor," he finished quickly.

"A witch doctor!" Nancy and Mrs. Porter cried out at the same time.

"Oh," he went on hastily, "in their tribe it is no stigma. Rather, it is a great honor. They believe some women have the power of healing. Your medicine had helped Abel. Therefore . . ."

So that was the reason back of it all, Nancy thought.

Now that she knew, the whole thing seemed a little less fearsome.

"What I don't understand," Conner went on, "is how they were able to make the preparations so soon after you were there. It takes time for them to get into those costumes, to assemble for the rites. It even takes time," he grinned at her a little, "to roast the monkey."

"Ugh . . ." Nancy said, drawing back. Then she remembered something. "I don't know for sure," she said, "but maybe this will explain their having things ready. Someone Abel knew met the bungo we were on. They talked for a few minutes and then the friend, or whoever he was, went off like a streak. . . ."

"That was it. The boy took the message, and everyone was ready when you arrived."

"But the . . . monkey. They wouldn't have had time to roast it!"

"Oh, that." Basil Conner was thoughtful a moment, and then he went on. "They undoubtedly had prepared it several hours before. More than likely they meant it for Abel's mother who, seeing she was being honored, might begin to improve. When you came, it was only natural to bring it to you instead."

Nancy remembered nobody seemed surprised at seeing her. Even the dancers had taken her presence for granted.

"They made a circle around us," she went on. "With the woman, Abel's mother, and me in the center. Then Abel held out a spoon and showed me with gestures that I was supposed to give his mother a dose of medicine."

"I hope you did," Mrs. Porter told her.

"Of course. Two spoonfuls, to be exact. And just as she swallowed the second dose, I heard Rex calling my name. The most wonderful sound . . ."

Across the heads of the others, Rex's eyes caught hers and held them, just a minute. No need to tell him how welcome he had been. Her actions at the time showed that, plain as could be. Remembering, she blushed a little now.

"I grabbed my bag and ran," she said. "Only," she added, "I left the bottle of medicine there."

"And she doesn't want to go back for it," Basil Conner said. They all laughed then, a laughter in which even Nancy joined.

"How did you know where to come?" Nancy asked, turning to Rex.

"It's as we told you. Miguel took us. Once we realized you were missing, he seemed to have a pretty good idea of what we should do."

"I didn't see him," Nancy said.

"No, he stayed there. I told him he should explain to them why you were so frightened." And then he added, grinning a little, "I didn't want them to think you were impolite, running off without even saying good-by."

Nancy tried to smile back, although, at the moment, she

hadn't cared what those people thought of her lack of manners.

"I suspect Miguel will be back here before long," Basil Conner said. "He'll want to explain to you people. The way he sees the incident now, it's a reflection on his ability as a guide."

At that moment a knock came at the door. Mr. Porter went to open it, and there stood Miguel. Behind him was Abel, looking embarrassed, apologetic, and frightened.

"Come in," Mr. Porter said, and the two walked into the room.

Miguel began speaking, so rapidly Nancy could catch only an occasional word. *Malo,* which she knew meant "bad," and something which seemed to say he was sorry, and others she did not even try to guess. Basil Conner understood though. He nodded now and then. Finally the flow of words slowed down, then ceased entirely.

"He says he's sorry," Basil explained. "It's much as we had guessed. Abel believed you had special healing powers and he wanted you to help his mother. And, as I told you, he thought that you, being what you were, would understand. A compliment, really."

One I could well have done without, Nancy was thinking.

"Miguel says Abel did not mean to frighten you."

The boy began to speak rapidly. Miguel listened intently, and then spoke to Basil Conner, who continued the explanation.

"He says he is sorry. And he wants to thank you for making him better and for leaving the medicine with his mother. He brings his thanks, and the thanks of his people, and the blessings of his family."

Nancy, deeply moved, nodded to indicate she understood. Then she went to shake hands, first with Miguel and then with Abel. They each bowed deeply, and both gave her a warm and happy smile.

"*Gracias*," Miguel said. "*Adíos*." Then he and Abel walked out of the room together.

Basil Conner was visibly pleased. The Porters could now see his confidence in Miguel had not been misplaced.

"You acted grand," he told Nancy. "Just real wonderful." He turned to Mr. Porter. "Now that Miss Nancy is here, do you plan to leave tomorrow?"

"Yes," Mr. Porter said.

Nancy turned to him, unbelief written on her face. "You mean," she said, "that you would have stayed here just because—well, because I was missing?"

"Of course," Mrs. Porter assured her. "We would have waited for you just as we would wait for Betty or Mark."

Nancy was still standing where she had been when she told Miguel and Abel good-by. Now, in almost too little time to count, she was at Mrs. Porter's side. She threw her arms around the woman.

"Oh, thank you," she said. And then, suddenly, she was sobbing.

Mrs. Porter patted her shoulder. "Go ahead and cry, honey," she said. "You've earned the right."

They were down at the wharf early the next morning, ready to leave for New Orleans on the United States mail steamer anchored more than a mile from the town. Here, as in San Francisco, it was necessary to go in small boats out to the vessel. And once they were there, they must climb rope ladders in order to board.

"I'm sure glad you're back," Mark said to Nancy. "I guess we would still be there—" he gestured in the direction of Chagres—"if you hadn't come."

"I'm glad too," Nancy told him.

When they were safely on deck, young attendants came to show them to their cabins. The one who went with Nancy said, "You have a good one. Not many people going back to New Orleans. When we came out—" he made a helpless gesture—"we were crowded like sardines in a can. All we could do to draw a good deep breath. Here you are now. Just across from your friends." He opened the door and stood aside for her to enter.

The cabin was small, but the bunk looked clean and comfortable. There was a cupboard where she could put her clothes. A kerosene lamp hung from a hook in the ceiling. Through portholes she could see the water.

"If there is anything we can do to help you, let us know," he said, and handed her the key. She took it and thanked him, thinking that she would not need a key now as she had needed one on the trip from San Francisco. She found herself wondering about the Courtneys. What had they done when they discovered she was no longer on the ship? What would happen, if anything, when they finally arrived in New Orleans?

She brushed the thought aside quickly and went out on deck. Betty and Mark came to join her, and they stood together at the rail, watching the white sandy beach of Chagres as they steamed slowly away. Palm trees lined the sand bar; the green tropical vegetation grew on both sides of the river.

"It looks pretty, doesn't it," Betty said. And then she added quickly, "But I'm glad we are leaving."

"So am I," Mark told her. "This is a nice boat. Say, did you know they have chickens on it? And a cow? And I think maybe some goats."

Betty looked at him, surprised.

"They do. I asked one of the—" he hesitated, not quite knowing what name to apply to his informer. "I asked one of the men working outside. He said they were for us to eat."

At least Mark and Betty will keep things lively, Nancy was thinking. I won't be lonesome or bored on the way to New Orleans.

"I'm going to my cabin," Nancy said, and left them standing at the rail.

She went inside and, once there, opened her bag. It seemed half an eternity since she had packed it back in

Panama City, making the difficult decisions as to what she should take, what to leave for Pacho. Now she turned her attention to the things she had brought with her.

Not many, and that was a fact. However, she had not started from home with a large wardrobe. Papa had told them they wouldn't need fine clothes while traveling in a wagon train. It wasn't important in San Francisco either, where she and Mama rarely left the house except to shop for groceries. Nor had she thought of what she wore on the ship to Panama City, and certainly not on the way across the Isthmus. During this time they had scarcely bothered to change clothes at all and were able to make only motions of keeping themselves clean.

She took her dresses from the bag, looking at them thoughtfully. On the bottom was the flowered challis, one of her favorites. That she knew without question should be saved for New Orleans. There were several she had worn in San Francisco, including the pink one and the blue one that Jim and Frank, as well as the others who came for meals, had seemed to think were pretty. She made a separate pile of the plain homespun ones she had worn during the overland trip and on the ship. With these she put the one she had worn across the Isthmus. These she would wash and freshen up as best she could. She shook out the others and hung them in her closet. They were not too wrinkled, considering the distance they had traveled and the crowded space they had occupied.

She placed the reticule in the bottom of the closet, realizing that for the first time since she left San Francisco she felt no concern for its contents. She would continue to take reasonable care of it, but certainly she would not have it on her mind constantly.

She bathed carefully, thinking how good it was to have a basin and water and soap and a towel. She bent her head so that her hair almost touched the floor and began brushing it with long, careful strokes. Finally she stood straight once more and let it fall across her shoulders, twisting some strands around her fingers, making a few curls to frame her face. She considered the dresses in the closet and finally decided on the pink one. The young man who showed her to her cabin had said there weren't many passengers aboard, but still she should give thought to her appearance. Be honest, she told herself. You want to look your best because of Rex.

Once she was dressed, she went up on deck. Mark and Betty, who had been standing with Rex, ran to meet her.

"You sure do look pretty," Mark told her.

"Smart brother I have," Rex said. Nancy felt her cheeks growing pink, feeling happy with the comment.

"Gee," Mark said, "Your cheeks are the color of your dress."

After the experience of the past week, being on the mail steamer was pure delight. As the steward had said, there were few other passengers. A man named Olsen, modestly proud of the sizeable fortune he had accumulated in California. Some men connected with the railroad being built across the Isthmus.

"Be finished, for sure, by '55," they told anyone who cared to listen.

A woman who said her name was Mrs. Morrison agreed with them. Her husband was there now, checking on some details, and he too, had felt sure of the date. There were a few others on the steamer, both men and women who, for reasons best known to themselves, gave little or no information about their business. Of course there were the Captain and the crew and the young men who acted as waiters and deck hands and did whatever work was necessary.

Nancy slept long and well in her comfortable bunk. In the daytime she sat in a chair on deck, watching the sun shining bright and clear on the blue water. Each evening a flaming sunset lighted the sky with unbelievable colors.

She had been more than right in thinking that with Mark and Betty on board she would not lack for company. They ran to meet her whenever she came on deck. Always she welcomed them. For their own sakes, of course. But also for another reason she almost refused to admit, even to herself. When she was with them, she could avoid being alone with Rex.

What an idiot she had made of herself the night he had come to Abel's for her. Hanging on to him as if she never meant to turn loose. Never, as long as she lived. She had been reasonably calm until she heard his voice. Was there something about deliverance from danger that made one give way more completely than did the presence of danger itself? Whatever was back of her actions, she felt now she couldn't face him until he had time to forget, just a little, the foolish way she had acted.

He must have sensed what she was thinking, for one day when she was sitting alone on the deck he came to her. Mark and Betty were in earnest conversation with the Captain concerning the way the vessel was kept afloat. Mrs. Porter said she wanted to go to her cabin and rest. When Nancy saw Rex standing there beside her chair, she made an involuntary motion, as if she meant to leave. He put out his hand to restrain her.

"Sit down Nancy," he told her. He took the chair next to her. "What's wrong?" he asked.

"I . . ." she began, and then stopped.

"Go ahead and tell me. I'll understand."

"All right. I can't forget what an idiot I made of myself at Abel's . . ."

"Oh, that . . ." He seemed relieved. "Believe me, I would have thought less of you had you not acted as you did. By the way, my mother said you first thought of going around the Horn and then decided to come across the Isthmus."

There was curiosity in his voice; he was obviously wondering, as Mrs. Porter had, why she had changed her mind. Suddenly she knew she must tell him. It was an explanation she owed herself as well as him.

"Yes, I did intend to go around the Horn. But . . ."

She went back to the beginning. Jim and Frank finding the house for them. Mama serving meals there. The sack left for Zeke. The man, Mr. Courtney (only of course she didn't know who he was at the time), trying to get it. Mrs. Courtney coming to insist Nancy stay with her. The ransacking of the house the first time she left it after Mama's death. Jim and Frank's explanation of the reason for someone wanting the sack of nuggets. And, finally, their insistence that she leave San Francisco, feeling it was not safe for her to stay.

"So they got passage for me on the ship. And there were your mother and Betty and Mark."

Rex was regarding her intently, not missing a word. What a relief it was to tell him.

"Then I found out that Mr. Courtney was on the ship and that he was the man who had tried to get the sack of nuggets by pretending he was Zeke's friend. Well—not really the nuggets, but the map he thought was in the sack."

"Yes . . ." Rex said encouragingly.

"So I decided I'd ask your mother if I could go across the Isthmus with her and the rest of the family. Only, I didn't think it was right to tell her about the Courtneys. She had enough problems of her own. Besides, I was afraid they might—well—start bothering her too if I was with her."

Rex's eyes were on her, direct and questioning.

"I mean," she said, "that's the way it looked to me. I could have been mistaken."

He was quiet for so long that Nancy wondered if he

meant to answer her at all. Or perhaps had not been listening. Finally he spoke.

"Nancy," he said, "I'm glad you told me this. It clears up a lot of things."

She looked at him gratefully. At least he didn't seem to think she acted silly or had been a big baby, afraid of her shadow.

"I believe you did right," he went on. "About deciding to come across the Isthmus, I mean. Offhand, though, I doubt that Mr. Courtney would have done you any real harm."

And, as she started to protest, he said, "Oh, I know he gave you every reason to be afraid. You were a girl, alone, with no one to turn to. I saw a lot of men like he seemed to be. Sneaky. Sort of stupid, really. They came to California perfectly sure they were going to find great fortunes, without in the least knowing how to go about doing it."

Nancy was listening, trying to follow what he was saying, only half believing him.

"A coward, that's what he was. Sending his wife to make the contacts with you after he himself had been unable to convince you he was Zeke's friend. Hiding in his cabin on the ship, still thinking if he could only get his hands on the map he'd have a fortune. He didn't seem to realize that, even if he did have the map, he'd be months making the trip back to California, and by the time he arrived, the lode would probably have been mined out."

Nancy was beginning to understand. She could even

bring herself to feel a little sorry for Mr. Courtney who didn't know real facts when he saw them, or knowing, refused to face them.

"My father didn't find as much gold as he had hoped for when he went out to California," Rex went on. "So, he decided to go back with what he did have. He was smart enough not to keep on chasing a dream that couldn't come true."

Maybe it takes real courage to admit your dreams were nothing but dreams, Nancy was thinking. Running away is easy; going back takes courage.

"I guess the really brave person will confess he didn't find all the wondeful stuff he was looking for," Nancy said, thinking out loud.

Rex looked at her keenly, as if he wondered how she had figured that out.

"My father was one to go wandering about," she continued. "Finally he met my mother and decided to settle down in a place that was nothing more than a wide spot in the road. Then he had the idea of going to California."

They were both quiet. It was Rex who broke the silence.

"I didn't know your father, but from the things you've said about him he sounds pretty fine to me. We need people who push on. Columbus wasn't exactly a stay-at-home. Neither were the Pilgrims on the Mayflower. My grandparents came to Missouri before it was a state. They all had dreams of some sort and set out to make them come true. That's different from chasing rainbows."

Papa was like that. Always pushing on. From Ireland to

Mexico and then to New Orleans and Illinois. And finally, to California.

And Nancy herself. Illinois and California. Then to Panama City and across the Isthmus. New Orleans next, and Cousin Matilda Hogan.

How long since she had thought of Cousin Matilda! Events in the last troubled weeks had quite driven the woman out of Nancy's mind. Now her heart reached out ahead. Papa had said any of them would have a warm welcome from Cousin Matilda. Nancy felt comforted. The Porters had a home in Missouri. She herself had Cousin Matilda.

Mark and Betty came racing across the deck now. "This ship is fun," they said. "The Captain has been showing us around. It's like having lessons, only better."

"Why Mark," Betty spoke severely. "How terrible."

Then, realizing what he had said, he put his hand over his mouth and looked sideways at Nancy. "I'm sorry," he mumbled.

"Oh, I know what you mean," Nancy said. "Don't feel bad."

"We'll go to school when it starts this fall," Betty told her. "But it won't be as good as lessons with you. I wish you were going to be our teacher."

And Mark said, "Me too," plainly hoping he had made up for his careless remark.

"I wish I were too," Nancy told them. "You made me see how much fun it could be." She knew she was telling the truth. Teaching was fun. Twice she had tried it, first with Don and then with Betty and Mark. Both times had been delightful.

It became a part of the day's pattern for Rex to stop for a chat with Nancy. She found being with him helped her sort out her own thoughts. It was a relief to talk about Illinois where Papa had taken care of everything, laughing and making jokes. And Mama, laughing with him. Then, Papa was gone and Nancy had to take over a great deal of responsibility. She found herself telling Rex about it.

"That happened to me, too," Rex told her. "When Papa decided he would go home by way of the Isthmus, people who had made the trip told us we should have every detail worked out before we started. So he decided we'd leave Mama and Mark and Betty with friends in San Francisco while Papa and I went down to Panama City to make the arrangements. That was very important, we were told. Unless you had things worked out ahead of time—guides hired and arrangements made about places to stay nights and so on—it could take weeks to make the trip. Then Papa was sick and I had to take over."

He paused, evidently remembering the difficult time. "I guess I grew up then," he said, seeming to talk more to himself than to her.

When he went on, he spoke in an entirely different vein.

"Because Mama waited," he said, "she met you." He made it sound as if that was the best part of all.

"I can't begin to tell you how much that meant to me," Nancy told him.

"Really, it's all worked out well, in spite of the way things looked at times," Rex said. "Papa can go back now and buy the farm. That's what he's wanted to do for a long time. He likes farming."

"But you don't," Nancy said.

"How did you know?" He faced her quickly.

"Oh," she told him, "I just guessed."

"But I hadn't said a thing."

"You didn't need to. Remember, Abel thought I was a witch."

They laughed together then, recalling something which had been far from funny at the time it happened.

Rex went on, speaking seriously now. "No, as a matter of fact, I don't. Oh, there's nothing wrong with it for those who want it. But it's not for me."

He was silent a moment and then continued, answering the question Nancy wanted to ask but didn't quite dare.

"What I really want to do is go to school. I think I told you about my uncle's school. Really, there are two. One for boys and another called a Young Ladies' Seminary."

"For girls," she said.

"How did you ever guess," he laughed. Then he went on, speaking seriously. "Because Papa found some gold he can not only buy the farm but hire help, if he needs it."

"And you can go to school."

"Yes . . ."

"So things really turned out better," Nancy said.

"Well, yes. I certainly like the idea of going to school better than digging around for gold."

"It's like the game we played," Nancy told him. "Remember—if you can't get a redbird a bluebird will do."

He looked at her quickly, his face lighting up. "Of course. And one verse says, 'I'll get another one and a better one, too.'"

"Maybe that's the way with a lot of things we think we have to have," Nancy told him. "If we don't get them, there's something else good waiting for us, somewhere."

Before he could answer, Mark and Betty came running toward them.

"Guess what," Mark said, "we get to New Orleans tomorrow. The Captain just told me."

It seems only yesterday, Nancy was thinking, since he was giving me the same message about Panama City. How long ago, really, and how much has happened.

Chapter 10

$\mathcal{N}$ANCY STOOD in her cabin, checking to be sure she was ready to leave the steamer once it docked in New Orleans. She had combed her hair carefully and put on the flowered challis dress, with its fitted bodice and lace collar. She would throw Mama's shawl across her shoulders in case the air was chilly, as it well might be since this was February. Fortunately she had a pair of shoes that were in fairly good condition. A hat? She had none. Gloves? A pair of Mama's she had not discarded, telling herself they took up no space in the bag.

And the reticule.

A bit on the shabby side, but that was not to be wondered at, considering the use it had seen. One way or another, it had been with her constantly since she left San Francisco, either in her hand or packed in her makeshift bag. She opened it now, touched the sack of nuggets and the container of gold dust. She counted the bills she had left and was comforted. Once she was settled in New Orleans, she would ask Cousin Matilda to go shopping with her, secure in the knowledge that she would be able to pay for the things she needed.

Cousin Matilda! The name seemed to shout itself to her, like a trumpet blast calling troops to attention. *Cousin Matilda Hogan.* What did Nancy know about her, really? Only Papa's description and the letters she had written, the last more than a year ago. Papa had been with her only briefly. Would she have acted differently toward him if he had announced he was there to stay? Her letters had been warm and kind, but people could write one way and be another kind of person when you saw them. How would she act toward an uninvited guest she didn't even know was planning to arrive?

Then Papa's words came back to Nancy. "If ever you need help . . ." Papa had a sure and instant knowledge about people. You could trust his judgments. Remembering this, Nancy was comforted.

"It won't be long until I'll see her," Nancy thought. "I want to look my best."

She felt in the reticule to be sure Cousin Matilda's last letter with her address in it was there. The crackle it made was reassuring. Nancy was ready now. She felt calm and sure. Just then there was a knock at the door. She opened it, and saw Mark and Betty standing outside.

"We're going to be landing pretty soon," they told her.

"Papa says you can leave your bag here in the cabin for a while. After we dock, we'll come for our things."

"Come on," Mark said as full of authority as if he himself were overseeing this entire business of landing.

Nancy followed them out on deck, there to join the Porters and the other passengers. The steamer was making its way up the Mississippi River now, with New Orleans spread out before them. A majestic white dome rose high above the surrounding buildings.

"St. Charles Hotel," one of the passengers volunteered.

The river and the levee formed a beautiful and shining crescent. The harbor itself was filled with ships, some of them coming in, some apparently leaving. People milled about on the wharf.

"Lots of business going on here," someone said. "Sugar, hemp—oh, you name it, and the merchants are down here ready to buy or to sell."

Finally the steamer came to a creaking halt. There was a great deal of excitement on the shore.

"Got the mail?" someone shouted.

From the steamer, a man called out, "Of course. Why else do you think we came."

The gangplank was lowered. No crawling down a ladder or going over the side in a tub. The passengers walked out on the wharf and to the white and sandy beach which was New Orleans.

"We're here," Mark cried. "We're here!"

A young attendant brought Nancy's bag to her; Rex

and Mr. Porter had theirs. No concern now, as there had been at Chagres.

"I think Rex and I will check on the next boat to St. Louis," Mr. Porter said. "Wait for us here."

Waiting was no hardship. There was an unlimited amount of activity going on around the levee. Vendors, most of them women, made their way among the crowd, many carrying their wares in baskets on their heads. "Pralines," one was calling. "Buy my pralines. Very sweet, very good . . ."

"Pralines?" Betty asked curiously.

"A candy, little lady," the woman explained. "I make them myself." She held one out temptingly.

"Oh, dear," Mrs. Porter said, "Papa has the money."

Nancy reached into her purse, feeling very pleased that she was able to do something for these children. It seemed she had done nothing but take from the Porters.

"Give me six," she said.

The vendor handed them to Nancy, who passed five of them on to Mrs. Porter.

"Oh, Nancy, you shouldn't," Mrs. Porter protested. But she took them, giving one each to Mark and Betty and nibbling one herself.

They were eating them, finding the candy sweet, crumbly, and most delicious, when Mr. Porter and Rex came back.

"Here," Mrs. Porter said, handing each of them a praline. "Nancy bought them for us—"

"—from that woman with the basket on her head," Mark broke in. They took them, began to eat.

"M-mm . . . good," Mr. Porter said.

"The boat?" Mrs. Porter asked.

"Leaves this evening. I bought our tickets."

"Nancy's, too?" Mark asked.

"No. Remember, I'm staying here," Nancy told him.

"Oh, I forgot." And then wistfully, "I wish you were going with us."

"Don't we all," Mrs. Porter said. But there was an absent-minded note in her voice. Plainly she was thinking mostly about being so close to home.

"We might walk around while we wait," Mr. Porter suggested. "See a bit of the town and find something to eat. The ticket agent says there are a number of good cafés close."

Then he looked quickly at Nancy. "What . . ." he began uncertainly. It was as if he had just realized Nancy was leaving them here. "I mean," he went on, "would you like to eat with us or go to your cousin's right away?"

Nancy had been thinking much the same thing. Would it be a good idea to descend on Cousin Matilda so close to mealtime? That's the way people used to do at the store. Mama and Papa never seemed to mind and always asked them to stay. But Cousin Matilda had not asked Nancy.

How could she? She doesn't even know I'm coming.

"I'll go with you," she said, making up her mind quickly. She could feel Rex's eyes on her. Did he suspect the real state of affairs? That actually she had never seen this cousin who had no idea Nancy would be coming.

"You can leave your bag here with ours," Mr. Porter told her. "Then we'll eat and walk around awhile."

"We want you to stay with us as long as you can," Mark and Betty told her.

They found the small café near the wharf and went inside. Without even asking what they wanted, a waiter brought them bowls of soup. Nancy took an experimental taste and found it entirely delicious. When the waiter came back she said, "What is the name of this soup?"

"Gumbo," he told her. And then, to answer the question he knew was in her mind, "It's made of shrimp and crabs and . . . oh, a lot of things."

"It's excellent."

"French," he told her. "Lots of French in this town. Lot of other nationalities, too. Germans. Irish. Oh, we have them all."

Irish. Cousin Matilda was Irish, like Papa. Nancy herself was part Irish. She began to feel more at home already.

They finished their meal and walked outside, without much thought of any destination. "Canal Street," a sign read. It was wide and grassy, with trees in the middle and narrow sidewalks on both sides. Omnibuses, horse-drawn, dashed up and down, taking people who wanted to ride on them. Hacks too, horse-drawn.

Everywhere were iron balconies on the houses, looking like delicate lace. A truly beautiful place, New Orleans.

"I think we'll go back now," Mr. Porter said after awhile.

They turned and walked toward the wharf, the place where the boat would leave for St. Louis. I'm not going to cry, Nancy told herself. I won't even think of all this time we've been together, the things we've been through. The Porters, too, were quiet. She wondered if they were realizing, as she was, that this might well be the last time they would see each other. So far away, Missouri, from New Orleans. So different their lives would be.

Then they were standing together at the counter where they had left their baggage.

"Yours," Mr. Porter said.

Nancy reached for it, but Rex already had it.

Mrs. Porter turned to Nancy, put her arms around her. There were unashamed tears in her eyes. "Honey," she said. "We'll miss you so. You've been wonderful."

Betty was crying a little. She stood on tiptoe, and Nancy bent to kiss her. "You're nice," Betty said. "You were a good teacher."

Mark put out his hand, as befitted the man he now thought himself to be. "I like you," he told her. "I wish you were going on with us."

Mr. Porter said, "We can't thank you enough, Nancy. You have been such a help, and such a comfort."

"Let us hear from you," Mrs. Porter said. "Do write, Nancy."

"I will," Nancy promised. "Oh, and I thank you. I thank you for all you did." She hoped she wouldn't cry, right here before everybody. "I think I better go," she said, reaching for her bag.

Rex did not turn loose of it, though. "You have your cousin's address?" He made it a question.

"Yes, here." She touched her reticule.

"How are you going?" Mark asked. "Walk?"

"I'll take a hack," Nancy told him. She pointed to a vehicle going slowly past them, the driver wearing a uniform and a hat.

She bent to kiss Betty once more, and then turned to where Mr. and Mrs. Porter had been standing only a moment before. Instead they were with Rex at the edge of the sidewalk, the three of them engaged in an earnest conversation, with Mrs. Porter doing most of the talking. Whatever she was saying seemed to meet with Mr. Porter's and Rex's approval, for they both nodded several times. Then they came back to where Nancy was standing.

"Good-by," Mrs. Porter said, kissing Nancy once more. Mr. Porter shook her hand and said, "Good-by."

Nancy said "Good-by," a trace of tears in her voice, and then followed Rex as he made his way toward the hack. He signaled the driver, who came over to where they stood.

"Where to?" he asked.

Nancy turned to say good-by to Rex, feeling that this was going to be the most difficult part of all.

"I'm going with you," he told her.

He helped Nancy in, put the bag on the floor, and then

got in to sit beside her. "Did you think we'd let you go by yourself?" he asked.

"Where to?" the driver repeated.

"Give him the address," Rex said.

Nancy took Cousin Matilda's letter from her reticule, read the address to the driver.

"By yourself," Rex went on, "in a town you know nothing about?"

Nancy said, "Oh," and then stopped. If she said any more she knew she would cry. It was almost like having him come to her that night at Abel's. She didn't know how much she had dreaded going alone until she found she did not need to.

They drove through the streets lined with iron fences and lovely houses. There were all sorts of trees and flowers. So much to see, Nancy felt she could scarcely look enough. Finally they stopped in front of a house.

"Here we are," the driver said.

The house was not large, nor was it small. Just average looking. Something about the homelike look of it reached out to Nancy. Already she was feeling that Papa was right. Cousin Matilda would welcome her.

Rex got out of the hack, reached a hand to Nancy.

"Wait," he told the driver. "I'll go back with you."

"Thank you," Nancy said, her voice not quite steady. "Good-by . . ."

"Oh, no," he said. "I'll go to the door with you."

They climbed the steps leading to the door. Nancy lifted

the brass knocker and let it fall. She braced herself. I wonder what Cousin Matilda looks like, she thought.

The door opened.

And there stood a man, quite young. Behind him was a small child.

"Good afternoon," he said.

A man. And a child. Cousin Matilda had no children.

"Yes?" He spoke a little impatiently, apparently wondering why these complete strangers would bother him.

"I was—I was looking for a Miss Matilda Hogan," Nancy told him. "She lives here."

"She did live here. But not now."

"Not now . . ." Nancy could only repeat the words blankly after him. It was Rex who took over.

"Where can we find her?" he asked.

"I cannot tell you. Not for sure, anyway. We bought this house from her about six months ago."

"Is she still in New Orleans?"

"No. She went to a cousin in Ireland. We had a letter from her. Jinnie," he raised his voice, "somebody here to see Miss Hogan. Did she have her address on her letter to us?"

In a moment a woman joined the man and child at the door. In her hand she had a letter.

"Good afternoon," she said. "You wanted to see Miss Hogan?"

"I'm her cousin," Nancy explained.

"I'm sorry, but she is gone. Here's her Dublin address, if you would like to have it."

Dublin. It might as well be on the dark side of the moon. Nancy knew her face mirrored her distress, for the woman asked anxiously, "Is something wrong?"

"No," Rex said, taking charge. "It's just that she didn't know her cousin was gone and of course she's sorry not to see her. Thank you. Come on, Nancy."

And then they were once more at the waiting hack.

"To the docks," Rex said. "Where the St. Louis boat leaves."

"But that's—" Nancy broke in, as the driver started off.

"I know," Rex said. "Now, tell me. When did you last see this cousin? Or hear from her?"

"I—" Nancy began. And then she knew she might as well tell the truth. "I've never seen her."

"Or heard from her?"

"Oh, yes . . ."

Nancy began telling him the story, finding it a relief to give details she had, until now, kept to herself. How Papa had come to Cousin Matilda's and found her a warm and friendly person. The letters they had exchanged down the years. Papa's assurance that, if ever any of them needed help, Cousin Matilda would be the one who would welcome them.

"So when I left San Francisco, it seemed right to come to her."

"When was the last time you heard from her?" Rex asked.

"About a year ago. Here." She handed the letter to him. He read it thoughtfully and then gave it back to her.

"She does sound like a fine person—one you could trust," he said.

"Oh, yes." Nancy brought the words out with a sense of vindication, both for herself and for Cousin Matilda. She was a good woman, and, had she been there, would have welcomed Nancy.

But she wasn't there. The impact of the knowledge washed over Nancy now.

"Did you write her you were coming?"

"No."

There hadn't been time to write. And anyway, it took a letter a long time to travel around the Horn, which was the way mail must go. Nancy herself would have arrived a long time before the letter, even had she sent one.

"It was all so quick . . . my leaving . . ."

It was then that the hopelessness of her situation came to her. The place she had been making her way toward ever since she had left San Francisco was not open to her. She was alone in a strange city where she knew no one. Except . . . And once again she remembered the Courtneys, who would one of these weeks be landing in New Orleans. Rex had said they would really do her no harm, but even so, she could not make herself face the possibility of dealing with them singlehandedly. If they still thought she had the map and set about getting it from her, how was she to avoid them? They'd find out in time where she was, no matter what place she chose to stay.

"What will I do . . ." The words held a note of despair. She felt almost as she had at Abel's, caught in a situation which seemed hopeless.

"You are to go with us," Rex told her quietly.

Again he had come to her rescue. This time she would not cling or cry out. This time she would use judgment and reason.

"I can't impose myself on your family, on your mother."

"Nancy," Rex said, "it would not be imposition. Remember when Mama and Papa called me aside, just before we left?"

She nodded. How could she have kept from noticing the earnest conversation?

"What?" she asked now, the question in her eyes as well as on her lips.

"She said if things weren't right—well the way you hoped they'd be—I was to bring you back. Does that sound as if you'd be imposing? Remember, you helped her when she needed you. You helped us coming across the Isthmus."

And I also caused you a lot of trouble there at Chagres, she was thinking. "What would I do?" she asked. "I couldn't stay at your house. Your mother has enough without me. And besides," she added, telling what she felt in her heart, "I wouldn't want to be an added responsibility."

"That you would never be," Rex assured her. "All along you have done your share, and more. It isn't as if you were a helpless child requiring constant care, needing someone to wait on you." She looked gratefully at him.

"But what?" she asked, still not sure.

"Listen," he said. "Remember I told you about the school for girls, the one my uncle runs? You could go there. And afterwards, you could be a teacher if you wanted. Mark and Betty keep saying how good you were at it."

Go to school. Be a teacher. Of course she could. She had the money to make it possible safe in her reticule. And afterwards, teaching. The prospect seemed good, although very different from the way she had thought things would be.

It was as Rex had said. People often didn't get the things they had set out to find. Papa hadn't. Neither had Mr. Porter. You did the best you could and then accepted what came. It was like the bluebird song. Through no fault of her own, all her plans were changed. But it didn't matter at all.

"I think it's a fine idea," she told him. "School, teaching."

The years stretched out ahead of her, bright and filled with promise. She smiled at him, a fine mist of tears in her eyes. Happy tears.

"You know," she said, "I think I like the bluebird best."

Rex reached out and took her hand, holding it tight. No need to explain what she meant. He understood. That was the wonderful thing about Rex. He always understood.

Author's Note

SOME TEN or twelve years ago, a friend of mine was talking about the people who, during the Gold Rush, went to California by way of the Isthmus of Panama rather than traveling overland or going by ship around Cape Horn. I was not familiar with this episode in our history, even though a number of important people, including Mark Twain, Bayard Taylor, and Jessie Benton Fremont, used the route.

"You should write a book about it," he said.

At the time I gave no thought to his suggestion. However, in the fall of 1967, when I was planning a trip to South America, I decided to include Panama in my itinerary and look into the possibilities of such a book. I wrote to Washington, D. C., for information about making advance contacts. I was given instructions on how to proceed and wrote ahead, telling what I wanted. As a result, when I arrived in Panama City, one of the secretaries of the American Embassy there came to my hotel and, driving an Embassy car, took me across the Isthmus. I even saw some of the rough paving stones which had formed a part of the trail traveled by California-bound gold seekers.

I also went to the Panama Canal Zone Library in Panama City to do research and to talk with members of the staff. There I discovered that some people also used the route for their return trip from California. Since I had driven in the direction taken by these returnees, I decided that, in case I did write the book my friend had suggested, I would bring my party home from California rather than take them there.

Once I was back in Amarillo, a friend of mine, Olive Caster Frisbie, gave me a brief written account of her great-grandmother, Susan Cody, who, as a young girl, made the trip across the Isthmus. She and her mother, a widow, went with a wagon train to California in 1849. The mother died and the girl, still in her teens, joined a group of people who were going back home by way of the Isthmus.

There were few details about her journey beyond the fact that she made it. This book is in no sense her story. But her experience did lend authenticity to the plans I had for my young heroine.

I read widely from many sources, finding that while material about people going to California was plentiful, there was almost nothing touching on the experiences of those returning by this route. As is always the case in any project I undertake, the staff of the Amarillo Public Library was more than helpful. I received information from the Library of Congress and from the New York Public Library, where I did some research in person. The Society of California Pioneers also sent me material. Of course I read *Gregory's Guide for California Travellers; via the Isthmus of Panama,* published in 1850.

I was fortunate in having help from some of my young friends in Amarillo who could speak with authority concerning my approach to the teen-age heroine in the book. Kim Finch read portions of the manuscript and gave many helpful suggestions, as did Jennifer Barbee, granddaughter of Olive Frisbie and great-great-great-granddaughter of Susan Cody. Anne Attebury brought to my attention Joseph L. Schott's book, *Rails Across Panama.* From it I gained helpful information about the Isthmus route, as well as the problems facing the people who traveled it.

I am also grateful to the members of my Creative Writing Workshop who listened to me read aloud portions of the manuscript and never hesitated to set me straight if such action seemed indicated. I am especially grateful to Rosemary Kollmar—friend, student, and fellow writer— for her help with Spanish words and phrases.

As I frequently say, "A book is many people." This one is no exception.

About the Author

LOULA GRACE ERDMAN is a Missourian by birth and
rearing, a Texan by adoption. She went directly from
the University of Wisconsin to teach, first in the public
schools of Amarillo, Texas, later at West Texas State
University in Canyon, where she is now Writer-in-
Residence and conducts an advanced workshop in
creative writing.

Miss Erdman is the author of several adult novels,
among them *The Years of the Locust* and *The Edge
of Time*. Her popular stories for young readers, many
of which are based on the tales of early homesteaders,
include the trilogy, *The Wind Blows Free, The Wide
Horizon,* and *The Good Land,* as well as *Room to
Grow* and others. She has also written many short
stories and novelettes for magazines.